MONICA ZEPEDA

BOYS OF THE BEAST

TU BOOKS

AN IMPRINT OF LEE & LOW BOOKS INC.

NEW YORK

TU BOOKS
an imprint of LEE & LOW BOOKS Inc.
95 Madison Avenue, New York, NY 10016
leeandlow.com

Edited by Cheryl Klein • Book interior design by Elizabeth Dresner
Typesetting by ElfElm Publishing • Book production by The Kids at Our House
The text is set in Chaparral Pro, Courier Std, Avenir Next, Gobold
Lowplus, Plump, OpenMoji, Throw My Hands Up in the Air,
Century Old Style Std, Arquitecta, and Averta.
Manufactured in the United States of America by Lake Book
10 9 8 7 6 5 4 3 2 1
First Edition

Library of Congress Cataloging-in-Publication Data
Names: Zepeda, Monica, author.
Title: Boys of the beast / Monica Zepeda.
Description: New York : Tu Books, [2022] | Audience: Ages 14 and up |
Audience: Grades 10-12 | Summary: "Three teenage boy cousins on a road
trip through California and the Southwest come to terms with truths
about their families and themselves"-- Provided by publisher.
Identifiers: LCCN 2021042916 | ISBN 9781643790954 (hardcover) |
ISBN 9781643790961 (ebk)
Subjects: CYAC: Self-realization--Fiction. | Cousins--Fiction. |
Automobile travel--Fiction. | LCGFT: Road fiction. | Novels.
Classification: LCC PZ7.1.Z466 Bo 2022 | DDC [Fic]--dc23
LC record available at https://lccn.loc.gov/2021042916

To Mom
I miss your hugs

PART I

PORTLAND

DECEMBER 29

OSCAR

Grandma Lupe shakes my shoulder until I wake up. "*Mijo*, you have to go now."

I rub my eyes. I don't remember where I am. Why am I sleeping on a couch?

"*Ándale, mijo*, you can't be late."

I sit up and look around. I'm in Grandma's house in Portland. When did I get here? Why am I here? "Where am I going?"

She hands me my Nikes as she continues. "He's waiting for you."

"Who?" I ask as I put on my shoes. Except they're not my Nikes. They're my old baseball cleats.

"*Ay, muchacho*, you know who," she scolds. She hands me my baseball glove.

"Where did you get this stuff? I haven't played ball in years." I look down and see that I'm wearing my Tigers uniform from Little League. And I'm ten years old again.

"Grandma?" I sound confused. What I really am is scared.

Grandma puts her hands on my shoulders. "It's time, Oscar. You're up at bat."

She gives me a gentle shove, and I'm no longer in her den. I'm on the baseball field in elementary school. The principal and two police officers are walking toward me. I can't run. I can't move. I can't breathe.

I wake up.

I am fucking sick of having this dream.

I really am stretched out on Grandma's couch in the den, but Grandma Lupe is dead. Her funeral was two days ago, and now I'm stuck in the house with my cousins. They're too busy with their own lives to notice me. Matt's writing in his journal, Ethan's texting, and Ruby's watching that damn Disney movie for the fiftieth time.

I don't even know who these people are. I've only seen them a few times my entire life. Ethan's bar mitzvah was the last time and Ruby was just a baby. The time before that was . . . I was practically catatonic, so I don't even remember seeing Matt and Ethan there. And the first time was for Grandpa Manny's funeral. We were still ankle biters, and I remember zip about that.

I pretend to still be asleep. I don't want to talk to anyone, and if they think I'm asleep, all the better.

Ruby starts singing along to the movie. I want to yank it out of the DVD player and break it into tiny pieces, but Ruby's a cute kid and I don't want to freak her out.

MATT

EXT. CEMETERY — PORTLAND, OR — DAY

A murky gray sky, light drizzle. CRANE SHOT over the cemetery, rows of stone tombstones and grave markers.

WIDE SHOT on a GROUP OF MOURNERS in a semicircle around a WHITE CASKET WITH A WREATH OF RED POINSETTIAS near an open grave, black umbrellas blocking faces.

A FALCON swoops out of the sky and lands on a weeping angel statue near the funeral. It tilts its head, watching the crowd. CLOSE UP ON THE EYE, so large it looks like a platter.

MATCH CUT TO:

A platter of tamales.

INT. MANUEL'S TAQUERIA — DAY

RUBY SHAPIRO, five years old, mixed Jewish
and Latina, pretty black dress, brown curly
hair barely tamed with a black headband,
carefully holds the platter of tamales
as she makes her way through the crowded
restaurant.

A Vikki Carr album plays in the background.
Bright colored *papel picado* banners hang
overhead.

The people in the restaurant aren't regular
customers but the mourners. There are many
races, but mostly Latino.

They are spread around the room, looking at
a collection of photographs on the walls,
talking and laughing as they sit in small
groups at wooden booths and tables, standing
in the buffet line with a pot luck of
homemade dishes.

Ruby places the platter of tamales on the

buffet table. AUNT SYLVIA, 52, Latina, fashionable black dress, stands behind her, a shadow we realize has been watching over Ruby the entire time.

                    AUNT SYLVIA
          Good job, sweetie.

Ruby beams at the praise. Aunt Sylvia picks her up and looks over at her teenaged son, ETHAN, 17, who leans against the wall in a secluded corner nearby.

Ethan wears an expensive black suit that's at odds with his baby face and brown curls. He's busy texting and doesn't notice Aunt Sylvia narrowing her eyes at him.

                    AUNT SYLVIA
          Ethan!

Ethan looks up, surprised and guilty.

                    AUNT SYLVIA
          Go see if Dad needs any help.

Ethan nods and slips his phone in his jacket pocket.

We follow Ethan as he passes OSCAR VARGAS
and YOUNG WOMAN laughing together in one of
the wooden booths.

Young Woman, 22, Latina, wears a black
sweater dress and gold hoop earrings, her
hair in a long ponytail. Oscar, 18, Latino,
wears a navy blazer that has a crest patch
on it. His black hair is messy and just long
enough to get in his eyes.

                    OSCAR
          Don't tell me you've already got a
          boyfriend! Come on, I'm grieving here!

Young Woman laughs as we continue to follow
Ethan.

Ethan passes another wooden booth with MATT
TRUITT, 18, mixed white and Latino, and his
MOTHER, 50, Latina, and FATHER, 55, white,
saying grace over their meal.

Matt wears a gray suit that is a little too
small for him. Mother wears a modest black
dress. Father wears a brown sport coat that
no longer buttons over his belly.

As Father says grace, Matt lifts his eyes

for a moment and takes in the scene. It's a celebration of life and a room full of love. There's a beauty in it that inspires him. He closes his eyes and says:

MATT

Amen.

I put down my Ideas notebook. I can't concentrate on writing the restaurant scene. I can hear our parents talking in the kitchen. Not words exactly, but voices rising and falling. The kinds of sounds that turn adult conversations into "discussions." They have to figure out what to do about the house, the restaurant, Grandma's old cat, and I'm not sure what else. I pray Mom doesn't forget to ask about what I wanted.

We "kids" were ordered to the den while the adults talked things over, but I'm not a kid. I'm eighteen. I should be involved. Not that my cousins care enough to make that argument. Oscar's eighteen, too, and Ethan will be eighteen in a couple of months. I think our parents thought we'd be close since we were born in a clump. But that didn't happen.

Oscar's asleep on the couch, probably stoned. I don't think he's been sober since he's been here. He smells like cinnamon breath spray, which doesn't completely cover up the scent of marijuana. Aunt Elena has no clue, or she excels at faking cluelessness. It's hard to tell.

Ethan's texting, as usual. He has the latest iPhone, and I'm trying not to be envious. Dad says having expensive things can lead to prideful thoughts.

I stand for a moment. The cat jumps up to claim the recliner I'd been sitting on and begins grooming itself. Our parents have been in the kitchen for so long, surely they have had time to discuss what I want. I position myself closer to the door, hoping to catch what they're saying. I do wish that Ruby would turn down the volume.

ETHAN

Me:

Ruby's watching that Disney movie
again. Kill. Me. Now.

Levi:

Portland's a cool place. There should be things to do.

Me:

You'd think. But stuck in house
with weirdo cousins.

Levi:

Customer! BRB

I stretch my legs and lean my back against the coffee table. Ruby sits next to me on the floor, bouncing up and down as she sings along to the movie. I look up from my phone. Oscar pretends to be asleep on the couch, and Matt hovers by the door. I don't think either one has said more than "Hi" or "How's it going?" to me since they got here. I'm not surprised Oscar's a stoner. That seemed inevitable. Matt seems normal enough, for a homeschooled kid, but Uncle Dennis is such a tool. He keeps telling us how much he loves Israel and how Jesus is the Best

Jew Ever.

Seriously, I hate being here. It's strange and sad being in Grandma Lupe's house without her. I played *Ave Maria* at her funeral, I was a pallbearer, I saw her buried next to Grandpa Manny. Now I only want to curl up in my own bed back in Las Vegas. Thank God for Levi.

Levi:
I'm back!

Me:
Have you decided what you're doing for New Year's?

Levi:
My friend Jake interns at Google. They're supposed to have the best nerd parties.

Jake? Who's Jake? Levi calls him a friend. Am I just a friend to Levi?

Mom opens the door to the den and almost walks into Matt. She looks at him with her eyes narrowed. I know that look. You do not want to get that look. But she doesn't say anything. She picks up the remote from the coffee table and puts the movie on mute.

"Moooooom!" Ruby whines, but Mom gives her that same narrowed eyes look. Ruby shuts up.

"We're ordering pizza for lunch. One pepperoni, one cheese, one veggie. That okay?" She's telling us rather than asking, but the cousins won't get that. Matt nods and Oscar raises his left hand for a thumbs-up, even though his eyes are still closed.

As she leaves, Ruby grabs the remote from where Mom dropped it on the coffee table. She blasts the sound. I go back to my phone. Of course Levi has friends. My problem is I don't know how to get myself out of the friend zone.

Levi:
What are you doing New Year's?

Me:

I hope I'm not still here.

I look up again. Matt picks up Mr. Taco and takes his seat on the La-Z-Boy. Mr. Taco grumble-meows as he hides under the coffee table.

Matt moves again. Now he's standing, looking at framed old photographs on the wall, rocking back and forth on his heels.

Me:

Cousin is acting twitchy.

Kinda freaking me out.

Levi:
Stoner cousin?

Me:

Fundie cousin.

Aunt Norma enters, and Matt's face is torn between hopeful and puking. She waves him over, and they leave the den. I wait a second before I go peek in the kitchen. He's talking to Aunt Norma and Uncle Dennis. I can't hear anything over that damn

Disney movie.

All of a sudden, Uncle Dennis hands Matt a set of keys. Then Aunt Norma gives him a hug and kisses his cheek.

Me:

Something just happened. TTYL.

OSCAR

Someone shakes my shoulder. For real. I open one eye. It's Ethan.

"We're taking a ride in Matt's car."

I open both eyes. "What the fuck?"

Ruby rips her attention away from the movie to say in a sing-song voice, "You said a bad word!"

"Sorry." I sit up and rub my eyes. "What's going on?"

"Matt got Grandma Lupe's car, and we're taking it on a test drive to Staples."

Ethan's wearing another preppy sweater today. This one's purple with a green stripe at the V-neck. It's the kind of ugly-ass sweater that's part of the uniform at Mesa Vista Prep, except ours is navy blue, and it's never really cold enough to wear in Phoenix. Pretentious douchebros wear them anyway, tied around their shoulders like a fucking cape.

Ethan's still standing over me, waiting. "You coming?"

MATT

Grandma's burgundy 1988 Ford Thunderbird Turbo Coupe is a classic now. Dad and I did a quick check under the hood, and everything looks solid. The tires show some wear in the tread, but they don't need to be replaced right away. The odometer reads less than ninety thousand miles because Grandma hardly drove anymore. It's such a relief to know that I have a car now, that I don't have to take the bus or coordinate with Mom and Dad to use the pickup truck. I've never had this kind of independence before.

I try not to be nervous as I pull out of the garage, but I'm not used to people watching me as I drive. I suppose there was no way I could get the car without Ethan and Oscar finding out, but do they have to tag along?

The rain has lightened up, which is good because one of the windshield wipers is useless. It swishes back and forth but only splashes the water around. I'll have to replace the blade before I leave for Santa Fe. But so far, the car is performing well.

Ethan sits shotgun, using his phone to navigate us to Staples. At least he's being useful. I let him put the radio on and don't even mind when he puts on an oldies station playing Eighties music.

Oscar traded the couch for the back seat and has fallen asleep again. I don't know why Ethan asked him to come along. We need shipping boxes for Grandma's stuff, but it's hardly a three-man job.

ETHAN

Oscar pushes the shopping cart like a maniac. He's swerving around guys in button-downs and moms in yoga pants. He makes choo-choo noises as he races down an aisle. He's going to get us kicked out, but it's hilarious.

Matt's in the aisle with packing tape, pretending like he doesn't know us. But then Oscar slides the cart next to him. "Whaddup, cuz?"

Matt's trying not to lose it. I see the anger in his face draining as he takes a couple of deep breaths. Matt is one very repressed guy. Either he's going to have an ulcer by the time he's twenty, or he's going to end up a tool like Uncle Dennis.

He puts a couple of rolls of packing tape in the cart on top of the folded boxes we'd picked up earlier. "Okay, we're ready to check out."

"Then what?" Oscar asks.

"Then we go back to the house." Matt says it slow, as though Oscar is unbelievably stupid.

"Come on, bro, we've got the car, we should do something."

I nod. "Something other than sit in the den and watch that fucking Disney movie."

"You said a bad word!" Oscar singsongs. I don't know what he's on right now, but he should take it more often. He's actually fun to be around.

Matt takes another deep breath. "The pizza will be delivered soon, and everyone will be waiting for us—"

"How are you getting the car to New Mexico, anyway?" asks Oscar.

"I'm driving it there."

"By yourself?" Oscar tilts his head like Ruby does when she's about to ask for a favor.

"Yes. I have a physics class at the community college that starts after New Year's. I'm leaving tomorrow."

"Bro," Oscar says, "we should go with you."

OSCAR

"We?" Matt blinks, but Ethan looks like he got lost in Costco looking for food samples and ended up in an aisle surrounded by tampons.

"We?" Matt repeats.

"Yeah. We." I am not at all fazed by their lack of enthusiasm. "We take turns driving, and we get there three times faster."

"I can't go to Santa Fe," Ethan says, still looking lost. "School's starting soon for me, too. When does your school start, Oscar?"

I let that question slide. "Look, we drive to New Mexico, Ethan and I stop off in Albuquerque and catch a plane to our own homes. You drive the last stretch to Santa Fe on your own. It's only, like, what, an hour from Albuquerque?"

"Yes, it is," Matt says, sounding like he's trying the idea out in his head.

I turn to Ethan. "Dude, this is our chance to get out of that house. Plus, bonus, road trip."

Ethan looks like he's making internal calculations, too. "Would the route go through the Bay Area?"

I put my hand on Ethan's shoulder. "It does now."

MATT

"Wait, wait." I don't know how Oscar took control like that. He doesn't say anything for days, and then suddenly he's planning a road trip with my car. "Our parents are going to have something to say about this."

"Sure," says Oscar. "We just have to make sure that they say yes."

That might be easy for Oscar, but he has no idea what I have to go through to get my parents to agree to anything. Do *I* even want to do this?

I take a deep breath. It's not a bad idea. Having two extra drivers would ensure that I arrive home in time for my community college class. And it would reduce the cost of the trip. I promised Mom and Dad I'd pay for the drive with my savings, but if Ethan and Oscar chip in some cash, then it won't set me back as much.

"You guys would have to help pay for gas and other expenses," I say.

"No problemo."

Ethan nods. "What he said."

"I don't know about going to the Bay Area, though," I say. "The quickest route would be through Idaho and Utah."

"Idaho and Utah? Don't you mean Armpit and Nowhere?" Oscar says. "We can go anywhere we want as long as we're in Albuquerque in three days. Isn't there anywhere you want to go?"

I take another deep breath. "I'd like to go to Los Angeles."

Ethan pumps his fist. "Yes! California for the win!"

Maybe this could work.

ETHAN

Me:
OMFG, I might be going
to Berkeley to meet Levi!

Jiwon:
How is that even possible?

Me:
I know, right? But I have a theory.

Jiwon:
I'm always in for an Ethan theory.

Me:
I didn't come out to my grandma because my
mom thought she wouldn't be able to handle
it. When she died, I was sad I didn't do it
because I think she would have been okay with
it. She loved me and wanted me to be happy.
It would be just like my grandma – playing
bingo with Jesus up in Catholic heaven – to
pull some strings for me so I could meet Levi.

Jiwon:

🙏 Thank God for grandmas.

Me:

Levi and I have been texting for six
months. It's not too soon to think
he's boyfriend material, right?

Jiwon:

Nah, you're in the sweet spot of possibilities.

Me:

That's what I think! The question is, does
he like me as much I like him?

Jiwon:

He'd be a fool not to be smitten. 😻

Me:

If I do meet him, I'll be as nervous as
Nurse Chapel around Spock.

Jiwon:

If he gets your nerd references,
he's the guy for you.

Me:

🖖

Jiwon:

#datinggoals

OSCAR

"Mom?" I stand outside Aunt Sylvia's childhood bedroom. Mom called dibs on this room since the Shapiros are staying at a hotel. The Depeche Mode and Duran Duran posters don't compute with the Aunt Sylvia that I know.

Mom's wearing earbuds, so I'm not sure she heard me. I knock on the open door. "Mom? Pizza's here."

She turns around and pulls out the earbuds. The soundtrack to *A Charlie Brown Christmas* plays faintly in the background. She's under the impression that it's okay to listen to Christmas music until New Year's. She does this every year, so I know to expect it. What I don't expect is seeing that she's packing.

"We're leaving?" I ask.

"Oh, honey, Tracy rescheduled my speaking engagements. She's gone above and beyond as a publicist making all these last minute changes, especially over the holidays. I set up a meeting with my editor, too, since I'm going to be in Manhattan anyway, and I'm doing some fundraiser thing for that congresswoman in Connecticut. Book yourself a flight back to Phoenix whenever you want. I'll be home after the Sanity Over School Shootings event next Friday."

My whole body tenses. I knew this would happen. This is why I jumped on the chance to go with Matt. I don't want to be on my own in Phoenix.

"He's waiting for you," I hear dream-Grandma say. I whack-a-mole that thought down.

"Me and Ethan are talking about road tripping with Matt to drive Grandma's car to New Mexico," I say, still standing outside of the room.

Mom smiles, the beginnings of crow's feet at her eyes. "I think that would be really good for you. You need anything? Money, maybe?"

"Uh, yeah."

"Let me find my purse. . . ." Mom rummages through the clothes piled on the bed. She finally finds it under some sweaters. She pulls a wad of bills from her wallet and puts her hand out.

I have no choice but to go into the bedroom. I take the cash and tuck it in the back pocket of my jeans, right next to the letter I've been carrying around for days.

She stands in front of me and pushes the hair in front of my eyes to the side. I wasn't planning to stand this close to her. I should've used breath spray.

"I know things have been hard, honey. We'll decide what to do about school when I get home. You remember to take your meds, okay?"

I nod.

She puts her hand on my arm. "Since your visit with Charlie was cut short because of Grandma's funeral, maybe you can still spend a few days with him when you get back."

Now is the time to tell her.

Tell her that my friend Charlie did not ask me to spend Christmas break with him and his family while she did her East Coast speaking engagements.

Tell her that my friend Charlie is really my dealer pretending to be my comic-book-reading, cross-country-running, peanut-allergy-afflicted best friend so she thinks I have a friend.

Tell her that the day I got kicked out of Mesa Vista Prep, I got a letter from Tanner Aaron Gibbs.

I have no right to expect you'll read this.

I wait too long. Mom's phone buzzes. She ignores it for half a second, then takes it out of her jeans pocket. "It's Tracy," she says, looking at the screen.

"Hey, yeah, I'm good." I can't leave fast enough.

MATT

It's too quiet as we eat lunch. The first few days at Grandma's house, there were constant phone calls from distant relatives and visits from neighbors and friends dropping by and leaving all kinds of food. But today it's just us.

We didn't visit Grandma often since we live in Santa Fe. The last time I saw her was about four Christmases ago. But Mom talked to her almost every day. I only talked to her once in a while and barely said more than "Hello" and "I love you." I'm not good at small talk. I feel like I missed out on something important.

"Remember that time when Mama kept Daddy out of the house because he was too drunk to find his keys?" Aunt Sylvia says to no one in particular. "He tried to kick in the door but fell and hit his head on a planter. He had to get six stitches."

"Daddy was only that drunk that one time," Mom replies. She delicately dabs a paper napkin on her cheese pizza to sop up the grease.

Aunt Elena snickers. "I wasn't born yet when that happened. Daddy told me he got the scar in the Vietnam War."

"I remember Mama sewed all our Easter dresses," Mom says, changing the subject. I can tell she's embarrassed about Grandpa's drinking.

"Oh, that gorgeous white chiffon with pink roses! I waited three years for you to grow out of it," Aunt Elena says to Mom. "But by then, I couldn't fit in it, either. Broke my heart."

"Chichis grande son muy buenas, mija," Aunt Sylvia says, laughing.

Aunt Elena laughs, too. "Mama always told me that, but I didn't believe her. At least not when I was thirteen."

I look down at my pizza slice and try to figure out the cheese-to-pepperoni ratio. I do not want to think about Aunt Elena's breasts. Yes, they are big. That is a fact. Let's leave it at that and move on.

ETHAN

Matt has turned the brightest shade of pink I've ever seen that didn't involve Barbie accessories. You'd think an embarrassing story had been told about *him*.

I never noticed it before, but Aunt Elena does have big boobs.

Mr. Taco works on the piece of pizza crust that Ruby gave him under the table. I think he has some problem with his teeth because he's holding it between his paws, licking it like it's a Popsicle.

That cat is older than I am. I bet Ruby's going to try to talk Mom and Dad into taking him home. She's not going to understand that they will say no because Mr. Taco is old and it's cruel for her to get too attached.

I scratch Mr. Taco's head. He continues licking the pizza crust, but he's purring. He probably doesn't remember he threw up a hairball in my shoes when I was ten. I freaked out, but Grandma told me he only did that to people he liked. That wasn't true, but I believed it at the time.

I want to text Levi, but there's a family no-texting rule while we eat. Ruby would rat me out if I tried. It still seems unreal that

I might actually see him soon. Ever since we met in the Queer Geeks room on ChatThat, we've connected in a way I never have with a guy before. It's more than liking the same things or having the same sense of humor, it's like he appreciates me for being me. Like he thinks I'm special. Or maybe it's all in my mind.

I sigh as I grab another slice of pizza.

OSCAR

This pizza sucks.

MATT

"Grandma Lupe paid the auto insurance until the end of March, and praise God, the insurance agent was able to add her car to our policy since we're with the same company," Dad says as I follow him into the garage. "But starting in April, it's your responsibility."

"Yes, sir." I quickly calculate how many more tutoring hours I have to do to pay for the insurance. I'm hoping Duncan can refer me to his friends, though I won't give them the same rate I give him since his mother goes to our church.

Dad winces as he bends down to put the insurance papers in the glove compartment. His back pain has gotten worse. Otherwise he would have insisted on coming with me on the drive to Santa Fe. But he can't do a road trip. He barely managed the flight to Portland.

"Dad?" I prayed for guidance on what to say to Dad about my cousins coming along, but now that I'm about to ask, I think I should have prayed more. I came up with a dozen reasons why this trip is a good idea, but all of them leave me now, when I need them. Dad is waiting for me to say something. I put my trust in God. "Oscar and Ethan want to ride with me to New Mexico."

He rubs his chin. He usually does this when he's stalling for time before he tells me no. I quickly start talking. "It's safer for me not to be alone on a long trip like this. They can share the driving, and they promised to split the expenses. So . . . is it okay?"

He taps his index finger on his chin. He hasn't done that before. It is disconcerting because I don't know what that means.

Finally, Dad gives a curt nod. "Of course your cousins may go with you. It'd be a good opportunity to witness to them. 'Faith comes from hearing the message, and the message is heard through the word about Christ.'"

"Yes, sir." I didn't think it would be that easy. I wait patiently for the *but*.

"Let's go map out your route," Dad says as he closes the glove compartment.

"Yes, sir." I am amazed there is no *but*. Then I remember I haven't told him that we're planning on going through California.

ETHAN

"How long is this road trip supposed to take?" Mom asks before she takes a sip of her margarita. After an afternoon of sorting through Grandma's stuff, we came to Manuel's Taqueria for the dinner shift. Mom's going to look at the finances and talk to the staff and customers after we eat. It's exactly Mom's skill set to figure out what's going on and get shit done.

"Three days."

Dad dips a tortilla chip into the salsa. "I was planning on flying back with you and Ruby on New Year's Eve."

How am I supposed to interpret that? That he needs me to help him with Ruby? That a few days difference doesn't matter? Dad says nothing else as he munches on the chip.

"I don't want you boys sleeping in the car. You can use your emergency credit card for hotels. I don't want to see any video-on-demand or minibar charges, though," Mom says.

"So I can go?" I sit up a little straighter in the wooden booth. I was pretty sure they'd let me go, but they made me work for this one.

Mom takes another sip of her drink. "You should get to know your cousins better."

"Cool." I look around the restaurant, which is super busy tonight. I feel dumb to realize that I never saw the cousins here for Thanksgiving. Grandma always closed the restaurant and hosted Thanksgiving dinner for her employees, past and present. Many of them had families in places like California or Guatemala and had nowhere else to go for the holiday. Everyone would bring a dish—pupusas, empanadas, tamales—foods that reminded them of home.

We didn't come to Portland every Thanksgiving, but we were here every other year. The restaurant was always packed with people singing and dancing, ranchera music playing in the background. It was completely different from the quiet, conventional Thanksgiving dinners at Grandma Rosie's. Now every year we'll be at Grandma Rosie's, I guess.

Dad scoops up another chip. "We trust you, Ethan. And we know that you'll tell us what's going on."

My heart stops for a second. I have not told them about Levi, and I have no intention of telling them about Levi. "Like what?"

Mom leans in across the booth. "I've told you how things were with Grandpa Manny. Growing up in a house with a functional alcoholic, we learned to pretend that everything was okay. I was hoping we could finally talk about it in the open, but my sisters are still in denial. And not just about Grandpa Manny. Things have been tough for the Truitts ever since Dennis went on disability, and I have no idea what Elena is doing about Oscar. It's up to us to keep the family together now that Grandma Lupe is gone. So if Matt or Oscar should mention anything we can help with, let us know."

I nod, even though I don't completely understand what I'm supposed to do. "Sure."

Ruby walks over to our table with our waitress, Serena, behind her. Serena places a terra-cotta tortilla warmer on the table while Ruby climbs over me to sit next to Mom.

"I helped make the tortillas!" Ruby claps her hands as Serena takes the lid off the tortilla warmer.

Mom smooths down Ruby's curls and kisses the top of her head. "It's a family recipe." Then she whispers over Ruby's head to me, "Family is everything."

MATT

"Why go through California? You add five hundred miles to your trip. That's almost an extra day." Dad stands over the kitchen table, which is covered in AAA maps. He doesn't trust GPS or Google.

"There's a blizzard headed for Colorado and Utah," I say. "I could lose more than a day, especially since Ethan and Oscar aren't used to driving in the snow."

Dad shakes his head. He spent too many years as a trucker to buy my best reason for going through California. "They're not used to driving in rain or fog, either, and you're more likely to get that if you take the I-5. Stick to I-84."

Mom says nothing as she sits next to me at the table. She looks down at her hands in her lap. She's not going to help me on this one. She knows when Dad won't budge.

I try another tactic. "I was hoping to visit USC. I know it'll be empty for winter break, but I could at least see the campus—"

"Matthew, visiting the campus is a waste of time if you can't go."

"I think I have a decent chance of getting in, and the financial aid people seemed confident I would qualify—"

"We think it's better if you go to a Christian university."

He actually said it. I knew Dad preferred that I attend a Christian university, but I didn't believe he'd flat-out refuse to let me go to USC. Now I know he was only humoring me when he let me apply.

I glance at Mom, who's still looking at her hands. Maybe he hadn't been humoring me. Maybe he'd been humoring Mom. She knows how much I want to go to USC, although she thinks it's for engineering. There aren't that many Christian universities with a film program, and if I got into USC as an engineering major, then I could still take film classes.

I bow my head. Maybe this is what I deserve because I was deceitful in my heart. "Yes, sir."

"Stick to the route, pull over when visibility gets too bad, and you boys should be fine."

"Yes, sir."

What am I going to tell Ethan and Oscar?

ETHAN

Me:

Glad to be back at the hotel.

Levi:

I'm watching Emergency. Have you seen it?

Me:

No. What is it?

Levi:

TV show from the 70s.

About paramedics. So much fun.

Me:

Sounds hilarious.

"Ethan, where's Gus?" Ruby stands by my bed with a panicked look on her face. I have no clue where her stuffed elephant is, but if she doesn't find him, she won't go to bed.

"Try the bathroom, boogerface."

Ruby dashes into the bathroom, and I check my phone.

Levi:

I'm digging the 70s vibe. And I have a

crush on Randolph Mantooth.

Me:

Autocorrect fail. No one is named
Randolph Mantooth.

Levi:

Seriously, that's his name. He plays one
of the paramedics. He's hot.

Ruby stands by my bed again. "He's not there, poopypants."

"How about the closet? You're always forgetting stuff in the closet." I look back down at my phone before she's gone. I quickly google Randolph Mantooth. I click on one of the thumbnail images. It's a headshot from the show. He's got Seventies shaggy dark hair, a square jaw, and what Mom would call bedroom eyes. If that's what Levi is looking for in a boyfriend, I am doomed.

Me:

He's older than my dead grandma.

Ruby slams the closet door shut. "He's not THEEEEERE!" It's something between a whine and a threat of more whining to come.

Me:

G2G. Little sister emergency.

I stand up and stick my phone in my jeans pocket. "Come on, Ruby, let's go search Mom and Dad's room."

MATT

I wish we could stay in a hotel like the Shapiros. But I've tried to make the best of five people sharing the one bathroom in Grandma's house. In the mornings, I wake up early to shower and shave before anyone else so there's still hot water. At night, I wait until everyone has gone to bed before I brush and floss my teeth.

I like flossing my teeth. I got the ideas for my scripts *Eden's Echo* and *Omega Point* while flossing. And at least four or five other screenplay ideas that are still in development.

Writer-directors have the most control over their projects, and that's what I want. To tell my stories my way. Stories that are thought-provoking and entertaining and can open a person's heart to God. It's not just the craft of filmmaking that I love. It's the personal visions of directors who make an impact on people all over the world.

That's why I don't want anyone banging on the door telling me to hurry up when I'm developing an idea. Plus, Uncle Martin says that in all his years as a dentist, I have the best dental hygiene he's ever seen for someone my age.

I don't have a story yet for the scene at Grandma's burial, but the image of the red poinsettias on the white casket stayed with me, and I had to put it in my Ideas notebook. Grandma's burial was one of the few times it wasn't raining since we've been in Portland, but I thought it helped set the mood. I don't know what the falcon represents, but one really did swoop down and watch us from a statue. It was eerie.

It makes me think about God watching over us. Psalm 121:8 says, "The Lord will watch over your coming and going both now and forevermore." I believe that with all my heart. I wish Dad would let go and let God lead me on the path He has in store for me.

Maybe . . . maybe I'm the one who needs to let go and let God lead me, even if makes me uncomfortable. Like going to California against my parents' wishes. Could I really defy them like that? Am I defying God's will if I don't go to California? I need to pray about that.

I throw away the used floss and turn off the bathroom light. The house is dark and quiet. When I slip into the bedroom that used to belong to Mom and Aunt Elena, I see that the second twin bed is empty. Oscar must be sleeping on the couch. Again.

OSCAR

I should get up and go to bed. Mr. Taco has been cutting some serious silent but deadlies. I can barely breathe. What was in that pizza Ruby gave him?

But staying on the couch means I don't have to share a room with Matt. He doesn't need to know about the nightmares.

OSCAR

I thought the kitchen was empty, otherwise I would've waited before I got me some cornflakes. Mom's talking on her phone, and before I can leave, she sees me. She motions for me to sit down.

"I made coffee," she says, putting her hand over the phone.

I get up and pour a mug for each of us.

"Uh-huh, yeah, got it, Tracy." Mom rolls her eyes at me before she gives two or three more *uh-huh*s and then a *bye*.

I put her mug in front of her and sit back down. I wonder how long it'll be before I have to say a word. Most mornings, she just keeps talking without me having to say anything.

"So," she says, "excited about the road trip?"

I nod because that's the minimum expected of me.

"I wish I could stick around longer to help with cleaning out the house, but . . ." Her shoulders slump. "I told Sylvia and Norma that I'll go along with whatever they want to do. We'll probably sell the house. I almost feel like I'm grieving for it, too. I haven't lived here in forever, but the memories . . ." She looks vacantly at her coffee. "I'm afraid they'll disappear. Does that make sense?"

I nod again. I am all about disappearing.

"I don't know what we're going to do with the restaurant. I think Norma wants to keep it. She's the only one who liked working there when we were growing up. But there's no way she and Dennis are moving here to run it."

There's a pause, and I think it's my chance to escape. But then she says, "Hey, is there anything you want of Grandma's?"

I am not expecting that. "Uhh . . ."

"I'm having some photo albums and Grandma's sewing machine shipped to Phoenix."

"You don't sew."

"I can learn, right?" Mom gives a small smile. "What do you want to remember her by?"

Before I can think of anything to say, Mom's phone buzzes. She takes the call when she sees the number.

"Yes, I'll hold for the congresswoman." She covers the phone and says to me, "Let me know what you want." She picks up her coffee mug and heads out of the kitchen.

MATT

"Road maps?"

I know this is the last item on the checklist. I put them inside the storage compartment of the armrest console. "Check."

"You are good to go." Dad slaps his hand on my shoulder. "I'm proud of you taking on this responsibility, Matthew." His hand is heavy.

I need to tell Dad. Last night I prayed about whether or not I should go to California, and I woke up with peace in my heart that God is leading me there.

"Dad?" The word comes out cracked. My throat is dry.

"Now, there's no reason to be nervous. I taught you to be a safe driver, and I know you'll make sure your cousins follow the rules of the road."

I rattle them off without thinking. "Pass trucks with caution. Signal early. Stay alert."

He pats my shoulder. "Especially that last one. You used to bring all sorts of books with you when you'd ride with me. I liked it when you read them out loud. Kept me sharp."

Both of us are quiet. He still has his hand on my shoulder. I feel his love in that touch, his need to protect me.

At last he moves his hand, but I still feel the weight.

He walks into the house. I follow him, saying nothing.

ETHAN

Me:

This might be the last text for awhile.

Levi:

But I get to see you in 10 hours!

Okay, probably 11 with traffic.

I smile. I am scared shitless to actually meet Levi, but it's also what I want most in the world.

Me:

I can't wait!

I pause and reread the message. It sounds too needy. I erase and try again.

Me:

See you soon!

I send it, then cringe. The exclamation point was probably too much. But it's done. I'm waiting for Matt and Uncle Dennis to finish their final inspection of the car. Oscar and I have already loaded up our luggage, a cooler full of bottled water and soda, enough snacks to stock a Circle K, plus a tin of Christmas cookies that Mrs. Kaminsky made.

Oscar's on the couch, pretending to be asleep again. The den smells like old farts. Not even Oscar's cinnamon breath spray can cover it up. I think about moving to the kitchen, but Matt and Uncle Dennis step into the den.

"All systems go," Uncle Dennis says. He pats Matt on the back. Matt forces a smile. He seems a little tense. I mean, for him. He always seems a little tense, but right now he's more on edge than usual.

I pick up Mr. Taco from my lap and place him on the La-Z-Boy. I scratch his head. "Bye, Mr. Taco." He purrs.

I know I won't be seeing the old guy again. Or this house. It makes me sad to think that they'll be gone soon, just like Grandma.

But, truthfully, the sadness lasts only a moment because I'm too excited to think of anything except Levi.

OSCAR

I wave good-bye to Mom as I walk toward the car parked in the driveway. I never told her what I wanted of Grandma's. I want nothing. I won't be responsible for more memories of the dead.

I slip into the back seat to wait for Ethan and Matt. I can see everyone standing on the porch.

Matt's getting a last lecture from Uncle Dennis while Aunt Norma hugs him.

Uncle Martin and Aunt Sylvia have their arms around each other as they watch Ruby make Ethan kiss a stuffed elephant she's holding.

Mom checks her texts. She looks up for a second and sees that I'm already in the car. She waves. I don't.

MATT

I pull out of the driveway. Mom and Dad wait on the porch, even though everyone else has gone back inside the house. I see them in the rearview mirror until I turn the corner.

Something in the pit of my stomach burns as I drive. I think I might vomit. I try to push the nausea down. That sense of peace God put in my heart about going to California is gone. I had that peace because I intended to tell my parents. But I didn't and now I feel sick.

I drive past the on-ramp for the I-5.

"Uh, Matt," Oscar says, "you missed the on-ramp."

Ethan looks up from messing with the radio dial. "What?"

"He missed the on-ramp."

I can see in my peripheral vision that Ethan twists around in his seat, straining against his seatbelt as he speaks to me.

"Matt, what are you doing?"

I grab the wheel tighter. I don't know what to say. All I can do is drive. I get on the on-ramp for the I-84.

"I didn't miss the on-ramp." My voice sounds ragged. "We're not going to California."

"Stop the car!" Ethan shouts.

My gut clenches as another wave of nausea hits me. I can't kidnap my cousins. I take the first exit and pull into a gas station.

"What the fuck is the matter with you?" Ethan's face is red from his neck to his ears.

Oscar pops his head between the two front seats. "Bro, chillax." It takes me a second to realize he's talking to me, not Ethan. "You should have told us if your parents didn't want you going to Cali."

I keep my head down. I can't bear to make eye contact with either of my cousins. "I'm sorry."

Ethan sighs. "Shit."

The burning that's in my stomach travels throughout my body until my fingers and toes tingle like fire-ant bites. I am ashamed because I have discovered that I am a coward.

"Okay," Oscar says, "then we go through Armpit and No-where."

"No!" Ethan's face goes from red to white. "Take me back to Grandma's."

ETHAN

"I'm sorry," Matt says again, his head bent down. His knuckles are white from holding the steering wheel so tightly.

"Matt . . ." I'm not sure what to say next. I shouldn't tell him that I only want to go on this trip so I can meet Levi. But I can't stop myself. "Matt, I kind of told someone I'd be meeting them in Berkeley."

"Dude," Oscar says from over my shoulder. I ignore him.

"And even though you didn't tell us," I say, "there must a reason why you want to go to California too."

Matt nods. "I want to visit the USC campus. But my parents want me to go to a Christian school."

He looks so sad. It must be hard for him to live up to his parents' expectations all the time. "I know what it's like to have to be the good son," I say.

Matt doesn't say anything. He doesn't move. He doesn't even seem to be breathing. I don't know where I'm going with this, but I keep talking.

"I know how important it is to respect your parents. Honor your father and mother, that's the Ten Commandments, that's in the Torah, too, you know. I get it. You have to respect them. We know you do. They know you do. And you can respectfully make your own choices, even though they may not agree with them. Your parents' plan may not be God's plan for you."

Matt looks at me with wide eyes, like I just read his mind.

"You're eighteen, cuz," Oscar says. "You're going to have to start making your own decisions sooner or later."

I'm ready to punch Oscar. Matt seems about to give in, and I don't need Oscar's big mouth ruining it.

But miracle of miracles, Matt nods. "Okay. We're going to California."

"Cool," Oscar says. "We forgot Twizzlers, so Imma go grab some, and when I come back, Ethan can tell us who he's meeting in Berkeley."

Shit.

OSCAR

I throw the little green tree air freshener to Matt as I climb into the back seat. Two-door cars are a pain in the ass. "Dude, the car smells like old lady powder."

Matt hangs it from the rearview mirror. "Thanks."

I stretch my legs out along the back seat. I bought rolling papers at the gas station, too. I still got some of the dime bag that I bought from a busboy at the restaurant. I'll be ready to light up at the next pit stop.

"What's the car's name?" Ethan asks.

"Name?" Matt asks as he pulls a U-ey out of the gas station.

"Yeah, every car should have a name," Ethan says. "Especially a first car."

"Wouldn't it already have a name?" Matt asks.

"I asked my mom," says Ethan. "She couldn't remember what it was. But she did say that this was Grandma's dream car. Grandpa Manny bought it for her on their twentieth wedding anniversary. That's why she held on to it all these years, even though she hardly drove anymore. It's yours now, you can name it anything."

"What's your car's name?" Matt asks.

"Betty Blue," Ethan says. "It's a blue Fiat 500."

"That's a total girl car," I say, "but fuck me and my gender bias, amirite?"

Ethan makes a huffing noise but doesn't say anything.

"What's your car's name, Oscar?" Matt asks.

"Chewy. He's a silver Jeep Wrangler, and when I start the engine, he makes the same growling noise Chewbacca does."

"Aren't cars supposed to be named after girls? Like ships?" Matt asks.

I shrug, but Matt can't see me, so I say, "Like I give a fuck," even though I'm trying not to curse as much in front of him. Another thing I've failed at.

"Come on," Ethan says, "we got to name this beast something. I was thinking Guadalupe, for Grandma, but it really doesn't have a Guadalupe vibe. Lulu, maybe?"

"That's it." I run my fingers across a thin patch of gray velour where somebody's head used to rest.

"Lulu?" Matt asks.

"Beast," I say. "It's not a sexy ride, but it's got history. Gotta give it respect with a name that makes it sound fierce."

"I don't know about Beast, though," Matt says. "In the Bible, the Beast is the Antichrist."

"In Marvel, Beast is a genius inside a mutant's blue body. In Disney, Beast is a socially awkward prince living under a curse," Ethan says. "The name means what you want it to."

Matt straightens up in his seat as he pulls onto the I-5. "In the book of Numbers, Balaam goes against God and an angel appears to stop him. But only his donkey can see the angel and refuses to move. He strikes the donkey, so God gives the donkey the ability to speak, and she rebukes Balaam for beating her. He finally sees the angel and is sorry for his disobedience. His beast of burden understood God's will before he did."

"Not really where I was going with that," Ethan says, "but if you like it, that's what matters."

"Beast it is," Matt says, looking pleased with himself.

MATT

EXT. INTERSTATE — DAY

Gray skies block the sun. Cars zoom along
the interstate heading out of the suburbs of
Portland.

The camera follows A BURGUNDY 1988 FORD
THUNDERBIRD TURBO COUPE rushing along with
the other cars.

Inside are THREE YOUNG MEN. The DRIVER is an
Oscar Isaac type, too earnest for his own
good. The FRONT SEAT PASSENGER is a Michael
Peña type, more a sidekick than a leading
man. The BACK SEAT PASSENGER is a Diego Luna
type, brooding and edgy.

As the Thunderbird heads down the highway,
SUNLIGHT BREAKS FROM THE CLOUDS. Streams of
sunshine blanket the road.

A FALCON flies high above the car before it
wings westward.

The Driver points the bird out to the
others. The Front Seat Passenger takes a
photo of the falcon with his phone. The Back
Seat Passenger shields his eyes with his
hand and watches it fly away.

I hope I can remember all this until I can write it down in my
notebook. There must be more age-appropriate Latino actors
out there I can find for the descriptions. I just can't think of any
right now. And I really need to find out what a falcon symbolizes
if I'm going to make it a motif.

ETHAN

Mom:

Have you looked in the glove compartment?

I have not. What could she have left in there?

I open it. Half a dozen cassette tapes fall out and hit my leg on their way to the floor. I grope around and gather them in my lap. They have hand-written labels on them like *'85 Is Alive* and *Mondo New Wave* and *Simon Le Bon 4Ever*. There are at least ten more cassettes crammed inside the glove compartment.

"What are those?" Matt asks.

"Not sure," I mumble as I text Mom back.

Me:

Are these your old mixtapes?

Mom:

Found them in the closet. Thought you'd get a kick out of them. It's a long trip without satellite radio.

Me:

I'm sure they are so rad to the max.

Mom:

Totally.

Me:

Thanks.

I pop one in called *Tommy's Mix*. "West End Girls" starts its techno beat. "Oh yeah," I say. "Pet Shop Boys."

"This was popular when our moms were kids, but what's your excuse? Other than shitty taste in music," says Oscar.

That statement cannot go unchallenged. "Eighties music is awesome. Best dance music ever."

Oscar rolls his eyes. "You a club kid?"

Mostly I do my dancing in my bedroom with Jiwon. But Oscar doesn't need to know that. "I get out now and then."

Another eye roll. "Whatever."

"What do you listen to?" I ask.

"I like finding weird indie shit on the Internet. Stuff like Dan Bern. Hussalonia. Dengue Fever."

"Never heard of them."

"That's the point. It's not force-fed to the public. It can be whatever it wants and doesn't give a fuck if you don't like it."

"Oscar, that is so you," I say.

"I also listen to bands like Queen and Pink Floyd and the Who. Now that's classic."

"I'd thought you'd be more into Green Day or Twenty One Pilots." I wiggle my fingers in a "gimme" motion until Oscar hands over a fistful of Twizzlers. I turn back to face the front.

"They're okay," Oscar says, "but I have my dad's vinyl collection, and it's mostly classic rock."

That shuts me up. Sometimes I forget what happened to Uncle Gilbert, but Oscar must live with it every moment. How could you *not* be messed up when something like that happens?

MATT

The music can't hide the sudden silence after Oscar mentioned Uncle Gilbert. It feels like a cold stone dragging us down into deep waters. I have to say something.

"The way Sam Mendes uses the Who's 'Baba O'Reilly' to build tension in *American Beauty* is the best thing in the movie."

Oscar makes a grunting noise that sounds like, "Didn't see it."

"It's overrated, even though it won an Oscar for Best Picture. It's midlife crisis angst, which is even more tedious than a teenage angst movie, but it's still worth seeing for the cinematography."

It gets quiet again. Duncan says I can be pedantic, or rather, he says I'm a know-it-all show-off. As his tutor, I should know more than he does, but he makes a valid point that my references are too recondite. And I probably shouldn't have brought up a movie that involves a shooting. At least if Oscar didn't see the movie, no harm, no foul.

I try another tactic to keep the conversation going.

"I like listening to soundtracks. Especially instrumentals. There's an energy to them and there are no words to distract me when I'm studying. I don't think I could have gotten through the SAT without Hans Zimmer's score for *Inception*."

"You know a lot about movies," Ethan says. "I wasn't sure if your folks let you watch them that much."

"Well . . ." I debate whether I should tell them that in fact, no, my parents do not let me watch movies that much. I check out DVDs at the library and view them on the ancient MacBook I bought for $85 on eBay. But before I say anything else, Ethan chuckles.

"Yeah, I thought so."

My hesitation was enough for him to get it. I had no idea a pause could be its own form of communication.

OSCAR

Ethan chuckles again as he scarfs another Twizzler. "Your secret is safe with us, Matt."

I like that my cousins have secrets, too. Not that I intend on sharing mine.

I'm not asking for forgiveness.

The best way to keep attention off me is to put it on them.

"Okay, 'fess up," I say to Ethan. "Who's this 'somebody' you're meeting in Berkeley?"

Ethan almost chokes on his Twizzler.

"Thought I forgot, huh?"

He sighs heavily, three or four times, like I asked him for money.

"Well?" Even Matt is curious.

"It's somebody I met on ChatThat."

"And . . . ?" I say.

"We've been texting for the past few months. I never thought we'd get a chance to meet in real life. So I had to come along on the road trip."

"Dude, we need more details than that." I'm enjoying messing with him.

"Who says you get details? That's all you need to know." Ethan bites defiantly into another Twizzler.

"Oh, come on. At least give us his name." I'm lobbing one in the dark, but I think I hit the target.

"Levi Metzger," Ethan says, in a tone that's a little defensive, a little happy to have an excuse to say the name out loud.

"Wait . . . what?" Matt takes his eyes off the road to throw a confused look at Ethan.

"Levi. His name is Levi," Ethan says more defensively.

"You didn't know Ethan's gay?" I pretend to be all shocked. Now I'm enjoying messing with Matt.

"Uh, no."

"You got a problem with that?" Ethan says, the most defensively yet.

"Not with you personally. Love the sinner, hate the sin."

"I appreciate your support," Ethan says all huffy. Then he turns on me like it's my fault. "How did you find out?"

I shrug. "Just kinda knew."

"It's the sweaters, isn't it?" He looks down at his sweater. It's red with gray trim today. "Jiwon thinks the preppy look is good on me, but I don't think I can carry it off."

"Who's Jiwon?" Matt asks.

"My best friend. She's first chair violin. I'm principal second violin."

"That I knew," Matt says. We all knew that. Ethan played at Grandma's funeral, and Uncle Martin mentioned a million times that Ethan was some big shot in his high school's orchestra.

"It's not the sweaters, dude," I say. "It was more knowing who the Pet Shop Boys were and admitting to liking them."

Ethan laughs. "Fair enough."

"Your parents are okay with . . . your orientation?" Matt asks.

"Pretty much. I came out to them last year. They keep reassuring me that they love me, they're proud of me, it doesn't matter. They probably say it more to reassure themselves, but that's fine."

"They know about Levi?" I ask.

"No way. They're not ready for me to have an actual boyfriend. I am, though. There are, like, four people who are out at my school, so not a lot of dating options there. Finding Levi was like winning a jackpot."

"You didn't say this trip was a booty call."

I can't decide if Ethan's face has gone bright red like a Twizzler or deep red like his sweater.

"I seriously doubt it'll get that far," he mutters. "Let me meet him first, okay? Jesus."

"Okay. And the name's Oscar."

Ethan turns around and wiggles his fingers for more Twizzlers. "Ha ha. You should get your own comedy special."

I hand him the last of the bag. Ethan won't take shit and isn't afraid to call someone on theirs. Good to know.

ETHAN

Me:

🍔🥤 pit stop in Medford.

Levi:

drool

Me:

Traffic has been

"Dude, you gonna finish those?" Oscar sits across from me, already eating the rest of my fries before I can answer. He disappeared for about fifteen minutes while we ordered, probably to light up somewhere.

"You can't get high and drive, Oscar."

"It's your turn to drive next, isn't it?" He licks his fingers clean.

"Yeah, but—"

"Don't worry about it," he says as he stands. "I'll be good to go when it's my turn. Imma get an apple pie to go. You want anything?"

I shake my head, but it doesn't matter because Oscar is already gone. I look at my phone.

Levi:

Customer! BRB.

I erase the text I didn't get to finish. What else can I write that isn't *See you soon* for the kajillionth time?

Matt returns from the restroom and sits down next to me. "How many miles to Berkeley?" I ask.

"About three hundred and fifty."

"I'll take the whole leg," I say. "Oscar needs to sober up."

Matt nods. I realize he's nodding over to Oscar, who is eating an apple pie at the counter while the cashier puts four more pies in a bag. "We should talk to him about staying sober for the whole trip," Matt says.

He's right, but I doubt Oscar's much for listening.

Oscar saunters over to our table as he attempts to stuff the Mickey D's bag into his hoodie pocket. "Let's *vamos*."

"It's just *vamos*. 'Let's *vamos*' is saying 'Let's let us go,'" Matt says.

Oscar laughs. "I'm so goddamn *pocho*. You should have been my tutor and maybe I wouldn't have flunked Spanish."

"What's *pocho*?" I ask.

"You're so *pocho* to ask that!" Oscar laughs again.

"It's Mexican Americans who aren't bilingual and are considered assimilated into American culture. It's supposed to be an insult," Matt says.

"I'm bilingual," I say. "But I don't think Hebrew counts."

Oscar laughs, a real belly laugh that causes him to double over. "That's the fucking funniest thing I've ever heard."

Some of the other people in the restaurant look our way.

Including two police officers sitting by the front entrance.

"Let's get out of here," I say, standing up and trying to act like everything's fine.

"The Beast awaits!" Apple pie crumbs fly from Oscar's mouth.

"Cool it, Oscar," Matt hiss-whispers since we're about two feet from the cops. One of the cops looks up from his Big Mac and gives us the stink eye.

I keep my head down as we pass them and go outside. We're almost to the car when I notice that the stink-eye cop has followed us.

"Hey!" he shouts.

I freeze. I've never been stopped by a cop before. I've never even spoken to a cop before, except in sixth grade when two police officers came to an assembly to tell us not to do drugs. I asked if I could pet their K-9, a German shepherd named Pablo. They said no.

Matt has frozen, too. But Oscar spins around and faces the cop. He's a young white guy with wavy black hair and a square-cut jaw. He looks a little like Randolph Mantooth.

"What up, police officer?" Oscar asks, smiling.

"Are you Oscar Vargas?" the cop asks, which freaks me out. How the hell does he know that? But Oscar continues to smile.

"Guilty."

"Yeah, I thought so. What are you doing in Oregon? Your mom doing a book tour or something?"

"Not this time. I'm here for family stuff. With my cousins." Oscar points at Matt and me. We finally unfreeze. I wave to the cop, which is completely dorky, but I don't know what else to do. What exactly is happening here?

"I wanted to tell you that your mom's book about community building is one of the reasons why I became a police officer. My brother died of an opioid overdose, and I wanted to do something to make a difference. When I read your mom's book, I realized that difference has to start with me."

"That's cool, bro," Oscar says. "She loves hearing shit like that."

The cop laughs, but it's an uncomfortable laugh. "All right, boys, you take care." He takes a step toward me because I'm the closest. "Is he driving?" He nods toward Oscar.

"I am," I whisper. I don't know why I'm whispering.

The cop nods again. "Good." He pats me on the shoulder. "Be safe." He heads back into the restaurant.

MATT

"What the hell was that?" Ethan asks as he pulls on his seat belt.

We have moved into our new positions inside the car. Ethan is in the driver's seat while Oscar sits shotgun. I'm in the back. It's more comfortable than I'd thought it'd be. Plenty of leg room, too. The driver's seat is a little low and lumpy. I mentally add a seat cushion to the list of things I need for the Beast.

Oscar tears open another apple pie. "It's no big deal. It happens once in a while."

"Cops recognizing you?" Ethan taps his fingers on the steering wheel. It doesn't look like he's going to pull out of the parking lot anytime soon, but I would like nothing better than to leave before the police officer changes his mind, arrests Oscar, and impounds my car.

"I was on TV a lot when my mom used to drag me on her book tours. I shut that shit down when I was fourteen, but people still recognize me if they've read her books. She always puts family photos in them. It doesn't matter if the book is about gun control or public policy or community building. It humanizes the statistics, she says."

I only remember what Uncle Gilbert looked like from the photographs I've seen, and Oscar is the spitting image of him. The same way Charlie Sheen in *Ferris Bueller's Day Off* looks exactly like Martin Sheen in *Badlands*.

"Why didn't you want to go on the tours?" I ask. I loved it when I got the chance to travel around the country on long hauls with Dad.

Oscar leans back against the headrest and sighs. "They're fucking exhausting to start with. Ten cities in two weeks, TV and radio interviews, book signings, school visits, all that crap. And I think she thought we'd bond or something during them, but it was like I was on exhibit as Grieving Son. My mom's fine with being Grieving Widow, it gives her a reason to get out of bed in the morning since my dad was killed. But I can't relive that shit over and over in front of an audience. So I told her she was re-traumatizing me and now I don't go."

Ethan finally starts the engine. "That's got to suck."

"If you only knew. People like that cop usually have a story of a loved one who died, so they think we have a connection, but they don't really know anything about me. And they don't want to know. They only want to tell someone their story," Oscar says, then shoves the last of the apple pie into his mouth.

I hadn't really thought about how difficult Oscar's life could be, but that doesn't excuse his self-destructive behaviors. I know other people who have had to face trials and tribulations. Duncan's dad ran off when he was five, and his older sister is addicted to meth. But Duncan's mom found Christ and while Duncan still hasn't accepted Jesus as his savior, he stays clean and works hard. He may not be good at school, but he knows how to fix things and works part-time in an auto body shop.

And then there's Dad. He's been on disability for two years. With his bad back, he couldn't do long hauls anymore, and then he couldn't even do short hauls. Mom went to work in the hospital cafeteria, and he took over my homeschooling. There are days he feels useless and frustrated and says things in anger. But he trusts in God that there is a greater good ahead for all of us.

There's always a path we choose to take. God gave us free will, and it's up to us to choose Him. And even though I know this path I'm taking right now to go to California will have consequences with my parents, I still chose it and I have peace in my heart again.

Ethan said back in Portland what I have been thinking, but didn't know how to put in words. My parents' plan for me isn't God's plan for me. I just need to find a way to convince them of that.

OSCAR

I should have bought a chocolate shake to wash down the apple pies. "Dude, hand me a Coke," I say to Matt.

He hands me one from the cooler in the back seat. I pop it open and chug it. I belch the alphabet all the way to *M* before I run out of air.

"Dude," Ethan says, like it's the most disgusting thing ever.

"Dude," I say back, "can't you see I need to practice? Can't even get to *Z* yet."

Ethan snorts. "When you go to college, you'll need to be able to do it in Greek."

"Like I'm going to be some frathole."

"Oh, come on," says Ethan. "Don't be judgey. I'm going to pledge Alpha Epsilon Pi, like my dad."

"You mean one of the nerd fraternities," I say.

"Again with the judgey. It's a well-respected Jewish fraternity. Mark Zuckerberg pledged Alpha Epsilon Pi."

"Nerd," I cough-say.

Ethan ignores me and asks Matt, "You joining a fraternity?"

"I hadn't really thought about it. Maybe. I suppose there are Christian fraternities."

"Yeah, sure," Ethan says. "Good networking opportunity."

"'Cause I'm sure Mark Zuckerberg is looking for a new dentist," I say.

"My dad has gotten plenty of referrals from his frat brothers. One of them is Jerry Seinfeld's accountant, and when Jerry had a filling fall out while performing in Vegas, my dad got the call."

"Wow, Jerry Seinfeld," I say. "Has your dad stuck his hands in the mouth of anyone else famous?"

Ethan throws me some side-eye as he drives. "You're kind of an asshole even without the fraternity."

"I'm just clowning you, cuz." He's got a point, though. It's easier being an asshole than actually dealing with people, but then it's hard to turn off.

MATT

"What colleges did you apply to? Besides USC?" Ethan asks me.

"Baylor, Grand Canyon, Liberty, and University of New Mexico. That's my safety school."

"I applied to UNLV—my safety school—University of Oregon, ASU, and the UC schools," Ethan says. "Berkeley's a long shot, but I'll probably get into UC Irvine, where my dad went. I can transfer to Berkeley after a year or two and then go to dentistry school at UC San Francisco."

"Damn. You think that far ahead?" Oscar asks.

"Why wouldn't I?" Ethan says. "I've got goals. Don't you?"

Oscar leans against the passenger door with his head against the window. "Dude, I don't even know what I'm doing next week."

"You want to go to Berkeley because your boyfriend is there?" I ask Ethan. I don't know any gay people, and I'm not sure what's appropriate to ask.

"Levi's not the only reason I want to go to Berkeley," Ethan says. "It's the best public university in America. And I want to live where there are actual seasons of the year. And Levi's not my boyfriend. We're . . . you know . . . friends . . . who flirt."

"Okay, that's not complicated," Oscar says.

Ethan sighs. "Yeah."

"Matty, you going to 'SC and become a famous director?" Oscar asks.

"Did you have to make a short film or something to apply?" Ethan asks.

"I applied as an engineering major. If I get in, then I can take classes at the film school."

"So you haven't made anything?" Ethan sounds disappointed.

"I shoot video for my church, like concerts and special events. They have decent equipment I can use, and I have a demo reel. I've been saving up for my own gear, but it's expensive, even used equipment off eBay. And there are so many other expenses I need to save for."

I don't mean to complain, but it has been hard, saving for college, for a car, for equipment, for a better phone—and then having to help pay the heating bill or electricity bill.

"What do your parents think of film school?" Ethan asks.

"They want me to become an engineer."

Oscar laughs. "Parents are the worst. Do they even know you want to make movies?"

I organize my thoughts to explain in a way that Oscar and Ethan might understand. "They do. But they're afraid for me. I get my parents' concerns about working in the entertainment industry. Even without the temptations of the secular world in Hollywood, there isn't any guarantee of success, no matter how talented you are or how hard you work. That's why I take classes like physics at the community college. I need to be prepared for the real world."

"But you've still got a boner for movies, right?" Oscar twists around in the passenger seat to look me in the face.

"I wouldn't put it that way, but yes, I want to make movies. My first memory is going to the movies. My mother took me to see *The Lion, the Witch and the Wardrobe*. I loved how the theater went dark and everyone got quiet. You knew something special was going to happen. And it did. All the excitement, suspense, happiness from watching the film—it was a physical experience you could have over and over with each viewing. And even at four years old, I knew that was powerful."

"So that's why Ruby keeps watching that Disney movie," Ethan says. "She likes feeling all those emotions again."

"Exactly! Watch it enough times, and you know when the big moments are coming. It validates you watching it again. As I got older and saw how movies became cultural touchstones, I wondered why there aren't more mainstream Christian movies like the Narnia films. Most of the movies made by the Christian film industry have so much bad dialogue and bad acting—and they seem to be only for the Christian market. Why can't there be a Christian director who can make movies like Christopher Nolan does—entertaining movies for the masses that deal with morality and the meaning of truth? I believe God has put that calling in my heart, and I just need to convince my parents of that."

Oscar settles back into his seat, satisfied. "You gonna go to 'SC and win all the awards and then your parents will be like, yeah, we always knew he'd be a success."

I smile at the thought, but it's a small smile. Oscar doesn't know my parents like I do.

ETHAN

It's dark and it's raining buckets and I hate, hate, hate driving in this. I take back every bad thing I ever thought about Uncle Dennis because I saw him put new windshield wipers on the car. Without them, we'd be dead by now.

It's not fair for me to ask Matt to drive when I told him I'd take the whole leg. Oscar's snoring in the passenger seat, and I still think he's not up to driving. But I really, really don't want to be responsible for four tons of potential destruction right now. I'm going super slow. Grandma Lupe probably drove faster than this.

I can do this.

Breathe.

Don't look at the lights of oncoming traffic.

What did I just tell you?

Don't look!

Focus on the red lights of the car in front of you.

Breathe, remember?

I can do this.

I played Mozart's Violin Concerto No. 3 in G Major flawlessly at the Spring Showcase. I scored a 1540 on the SAT. I read all seventy-two volumes of *Naruto* in a week.

I can do this.

I've got Levi waiting for me.

Only one hundred and forty-two more miles. One hundred and forty-two miles of darkness and rain and . . .

I can do this.

I blast the music. Depeche Mode's "Just Can't Get Enough" is exactly what I need right now.

MATT

Ethan sings along loudly to the music. Oscar wakes up in the front passenger seat with a start. "Hell no!"

Ethan stops singing. "What's your problem?"

Oscar rubs his eyes. He takes a long moment figuring out where he is. "I was having a weird-ass dream."

"What was it about?" There's a high probability that Oscar will brush me off, but I'm curious. There's more to him than he lets on.

He rubs his eyes again. "Grandma was taking me to a baseball game, and I didn't want to go."

"That doesn't sound weird," Ethan says.

Oscar runs his fingers through his hair. "It was . . . whatever."

"I've had a couple of dreams about Grandma," says Ethan. "She's watching television with Ruby and me when Mr. Taco jumps on her lap. Mr. Taco starts meowing because he wants to be fed, but Grandma tells him, 'Not until after *Jeopardy!*' So Mr. Taco answers the Final Jeopardy clue with 'What is tomorrow and tomorrow and tomorrow?'"

"That's from *Macbeth*," I say.

"I know!" Ethan says. "How random is that?"

I haven't dreamed about Grandma at all. At least I don't remember dreaming about her. I know that a person is supposed to dream four to six times a night, but I never remember my dreams.

No one responds to Ethan, so he keeps talking. "In my dream, Grandma laughs and laughs at Mr. Taco and we're all laughing, too, even Mr. Taco. I'm going to miss her laugh. She sounded like the flute in *Peter and the Wolf*."

Ethan is quiet after that. I don't know what the flute in *Peter and the Wolf* sounds like. I don't remember Grandma's laugh. I wish I did.

"Grandma used to sing," Oscar says. "Old ranchera songs and that one singer . . . What's her name?"

"Vikki Carr," I say. "Grandma loved Vikki Carr. My mom listens to those songs, too. Usually when she cooks."

It gets quiet again.

After a few minutes, Ethan breaks the silence. "I don't know how you guys managed to use the bathroom at the house. I flat-out refused to."

"What are you talking about?" Oscar says, sounding as confused as I am.

Ethan looks from the road to Oscar for a split second, shocked. "No one told you how Grandma Lupe died?"

"Her neighbor found her when she went to pick her up for Midnight Mass," says Oscar. "She had a heart attack. Probably been dead a couple of hours."

"But do you know where Mrs. Kaminsky found her?"

"In bed," Oscar says.

I nod, although no one can see me in the back seat. I even wrote out the scene in my Ideas notebook.

EXT. CARDENAS HOUSE — NIGHT

MRS. KAMINSKY, 60s, white, ruddy-faced and round body, stands on the porch and RINGS the doorbell. She wears a bright pink parka that makes her even rounder.

She peeks through the frosted glass window in the front door, but can't see anything.

INT. CARDENAS HOUSE — FOYER — NIGHT

Mrs. Kaminsky opens the front door and enters. There's a lamp on in the adjoining living room, but the rest of the house is dark.

AN OLD GRAY CAT dashes across the foyer into the living room.

She stands, uncertain, in the foyer.

                    MRS. KAMINSKY
          Lupe?

INT. GRANDMA'S BEDROOM — NIGHT

Mrs. Kaminsky enters the dark room. She flicks on the light switch.

REVEAL GRANDMA LUPE in bed. She's small, almost lost under a heavy white chenille comforter in the middle of the double bed. Her silver hair is spread out over the pillow. Her eyes are closed.

Mrs. Kaminsky realizes something is wrong. She touches Grandma's forehead, like feeling for a fever. She quickly withdraws her hand.

She makes the sign of the cross.

Maybe I should add a painting of a falcon on the bedroom wall to continue the motif.

OSCAR

"That's not how it happened." Ethan sounds smug.

"Either you know or you don't know," I say.

"She died"—he lowers his voice—"on the toilet."

"What?" comes from Matt in the back.

"Grandma died on the can," I say. The look on Matt's face is somewhere between disgust and horror.

"Old people die on the toilet all the time," says Ethan. "They strain too hard and boom! Heart attack. That's what happened to Grandma Lupe. She fell over and Mrs. Kaminsky found her face down in the cat litter."

I get why no one told tell us the truth. Death should not be that ridiculous. Grandma and me weren't close—our relationship consisted of phone calls on birthdays and holidays. But, damn, she deserved a more dignified way to check out. Then I remember something. "I rubbed one out next to that toilet."

The disgust and horror on Matt's face only increases. "You what?"

"Come on, bro, you've never rubbed one out in the morning? It's part of the morning routine, like brushing your teeth."

"I am super relieved I never used that bathroom," Ethan says, even more smug.

Matt looks stone-faced. "I find this conversation to be inappropriate."

I laugh so hard my stomach hurts. "I bet you do."

PART II

BERKELEY

MATT

"Why did you book this shithole if it doesn't have enough parking?" Oscar asks.

"Look, it's done," Ethan says. "Shut up and help me find a spot."

This is the fifth time we've driven around the same four blocks. There is no available parking at our hotel, which is bad enough, but the street parking seems to be permit only.

"Use the market parking lot," Oscar says. "It's right next to the hotel."

"They'll tow," Ethan says. "Levi says they don't screw around."

"I'd have to veto any questionable parking choices," I say. "I'm not getting my car towed."

"But, bro, we've driving around for twenty minutes, and I really have to take a leak."

"There's a spot!" I shout. A Prius is pulling out of a parking space only a block away from the hotel.

"Are you kidding me?" Ethan says. "I can't park the Beast there."

The parking space is between a Subaru Outback and a Ford Explorer. It'll be tight, but it can be done.

A car honks behind us as Ethan hesitates.

"Dude, take it, take it!" Oscar shouts.

Ethan slowly noses the Beast into the parking space. A line of cars quickly forms behind us.

"What are you doing?" Oscar asks.

"I'm parking the Beast."

"Are you shitting me? Do you even know how to parallel park?"

"Do you want to do it?" Ethan asks Oscar.

"Hells yeah!"

There's a chorus of honks as Oscar gets out of the car. It's just past 6 p.m., peak commuting time, and no one has the patience to wait for us. I watch from the back seat as Oscar comes around to the driver's side door. I try not to panic, but I don't know what to do.

Oscar opens the car door. "*¡Vamos!*"

Ethan sighs heavily as he unsnaps his seatbelt. As he exits the car, a BMW convertible swerves around the Beast and almost hits him.

The BMW driver shouts, "Assholes!"

Ethan and Oscar both give the BMW driver the finger. Then they look at each other and laugh.

The blare of horns has increased in duration and frequency. My heart pounds faster with each one. I can't sit here and do nothing.

"I'll do it! I'll park the car," I say as I body dive from the back seat to the driver's seat. I hit my shin hard on the steering wheel.

Ethan and Oscar are stunned as I slam shut the driver's door. I turn around with my arm across the passenger's seat to look behind me. The backlog of cars has grown, their headlights stretching to the end of the block. I wave to the other cars before I put the Beast in reverse and line up properly to parallel park.

I slide the Beast into the spot.

I join Ethan and Oscar on the sidewalk, watching as the backlog zips past the parked Beast.

"I'm never going to live this down, am I?" asks Ethan.

"Nope," Oscar replies.

OSCAR

"I stand by my first impression," I say. "This place is a shithole." The room is small and shabby. The balcony has a view of the supermarket parking lot next door. I throw my duffel bag on one of the queen beds to claim it. Matt and Ethan can cozy up together in the other one. I am not sharing.

Ethan shrugs. "It's the holidays. There wasn't a lot available."

Matt comes in and scopes the place. Ethan has spread out on the second bed. He's not sharing, either. "Two beds? Can't we get a roll-away?"

"Where would we put it? The bathroom?" Ethan asks.

"Come on, guys," Matt says. He rubs his shin where he whacked it on the steering wheel.

"Okay, okay, okay." I move my duffel bag. I know I'm an asshole for not doing any of the driving. "I'll sleep in the chair." I plop on the butt-ugly armchair in the corner.

"We can share," Matt says. "I'm not homophobic."

Ethan snorts.

"I didn't mean it like that," Matt says.

Ethan snorts again.

"The chair is fine," I say. "I'll take an Ativan, and it won't matter where I sleep."

Ethan sits up. "But you'll be able to drive tomorrow, right?"

Now I really feel like an asshole for not doing my share of the driving. I'm going to have to pull my weight because Ethan's keeping tabs.

"Yeah, I'll be fine."

Ethan and Matt share a look. It's the can-we-trust-Oscar-not-to-fuck-up look. Teachers, psychiatrists, Mom, I've seen that look plenty.

"Hey, I'm starving. Let's eat." I can't move the focus off me fast enough.

"I know a place nearby," Ethan says.

ETHAN

We take a booth at Saul's Deli near the back. It's exactly like Levi said. The red booths, the black-and-white tile floor, the framed vinyl records of Yiddish performers on the walls, the young hipsters and old Jews in an uneasy truce over latkes with housemade applesauce.

I'm about to throw up from anticipation. My phone pings.

Levi:
What happened to you? Flat tire? Alien abduction?
Cosmic time rift? WHERE ARE YOU????

Me:
Table 12.

A loud yelp comes from the deli kitchen. A tornado in a white apron appears and pulls me out of the booth and into a hug. I am in Levi's arms. He's hugging me and shouting something I can't even process because he's hugging me and we're jumping around together and I realize I'm shouting, too, but I don't think it's even words. It's a shout of joy, of relief, of happiness, and I'm not going to be embarrassed even though I see Oscar smirking and Matt looking dumbfounded.

Our chaotic happiness lasts a few seconds, then the shouting and the jumping and the hugging are over and I find myself sitting back in the booth. But this time, Levi sits next to me.

"You're really here! You should have given me a little warning. I would've changed my shirt. I smell like chopped liver."

He looks perfect. He has curly reddish-brown hair and freckles and a smile that lets you in on the joke. Under his white apron he wears a blue T-shirt with the Cal logo and jeans. Perfect.

"I've been on the road all day," I say. "I smell like McDonald's fries and Oscar's farts."

Oscar laughs. Matt still looks dumbstruck.

"These must be the cousins," Levi says.

"Cousin Number One," Oscar says, then points his thumb at Matt, "and that's Cousin Number Two."

"Bonding on a road trip after your grandma's funeral," says Levi. "That's so Eighties movie, I love it!"

"Which road trip movie?" asks Matt. "*The Blues Brothers*? *National Lampoon's Vacation*? None of them really fit—"

"Do any of them have John Cusack? I want to be John Cusack," Oscar says.

"I want to be John Cusack," I say. "I loved him in *Ferris Bueller's Day Off*."

"I like to think there's a little bit of John Cusack in all of us," Levi says. "We just have to be brave enough to unleash it."

"John Cusack wasn't in *Ferris Bueller's*—"

"Hey, Levi, you gonna let your friends order, or you prefer they go hungry?" The waitress comes to our table and interrupts Matt.

"Sophie, four pastramis on rye, extra coleslaw, and egg creams all around," Levi says. The waitress leaves, and Levi leans in to us. "Trust me, guys, this shit's legit! Gotta clock out, but be back in a sec."

And the tornado known as Levi is gone.

"Hey, Ethan," Oscar says, "he's okay."

Perfect. He's perfect.

MATT

"I like this." I've never had an egg cream before. The mix of chocolate milk and club soda is surprisingly good. "I don't know why it's called an egg cream, but it's delicious."

"Leave room for a black and white," Levi says. He sits next to Ethan, eating fries from his plate. Ethan doesn't seem to mind.

"What's that?" I ask.

"There's a serious lack of Jewish delis in your life," Levi says. "Black and white cookies. God's gift to the Jews."

"I thought that was Israel," I say.

"Israel, black and white cookies, then bagels and lox," Ethan says.

"Israel, black and white cookies, bagels and lox, and Bob Dylan," Levi says.

"I would've said Itzhak Perlman, but you weren't forced to play an instrument," Ethan says.

Ethan and Levi laugh. They've been talking like this through dinner. It's fast and comfortable, almost like their own secret code. You can tell they've been friends for a while, even though this is the first time they've met in person. Ethan is more relaxed than I've ever seen him.

"And God's gift to Mexicans? Tequila and tacos. Why aren't we the chosen people?" Oscar says.

Everyone laughs except me. I don't know why that's funny to them. Oscar has been joking along with them, like he's part of their inner circle.

"Is there a name for Latino Jews?" Oscar says. "Jewtino? Hebspanic? Wait, wait, I got it . . . Chican-*oy!*"

"Those are all really, really awful," Ethan says. "Can I not be related to you?"

Everyone laughs again. Except me. How does Oscar say such obnoxious things and get away with it?

"Where's the bathroom?" I ask.

Levi points to the back. I'm almost there when I hear them laugh again.

ETHAN

"Make sure you include the employee discount," Levi says to our waitress as she puts the bill down on the table.

"You make sure these guys don't leave a shit tip," she says, smiling a half-serious smile.

"I got it," Oscar says, taking the bill.

"We're supposed to split expenses," I say. "And Matt's not back yet."

Oscar shrugs and goes to the counter to pay.

"He doesn't seem as flaky as you said," Levi whispers.

"He's . . . what he wants to be when he wants to be, I guess," I whisper back.

"His dad saved those students from a school shooter, right?"

"Yeah, the shooter held my uncle's classroom hostage for hours, and when some kids finally tried to rush the guy, Uncle Gilbert jumped in and took the fire. The shooter gave himself up after that."

"Wasn't he recently released on probation?" Levi lowers his voice even more.

"I hadn't heard that." I lower my voice too, even though

Oscar's still gone. "But how can he be released? He shot two kids and killed my uncle. And he killed his dad, too, before that. I remember his defense attorney made a big deal about how his dad was super abusive and a doomsday prepper about to take the family off the grid to a compound in Idaho. Maybe that's why he got released? I know the case was up for appeal."

"I think it was because he was fourteen at the time and tried as a juvenile. Something like that," Levi says.

"That's messed up." We're so close, our shoulders touching, our faces inches apart. I don't want to think about the shitty life of a school shooter. I want to know what Levi's lips feel like.

"You were spot-on about your other cousin, though," he says.

I shake my head to get rid of the thought of Levi's lips. "Yeah, Matt's a little uptight but he's kind of—" I see Matt returning from the bathroom and I shut up.

Oscar comes back to the table the same time as Matt and hands each of us a black and white cookie. "Mazel tov," he says, saluting us with his own cookie. Then he takes a bite. "Oh my god, these are even better than Mickey D apple pies."

Matt inspects his cookie closely. "Oh, sure, black and white." He takes a big bite. "Mmmm, gof," he manages through crumbs.

Levi pats him on the back. "Attaboy."

We walk out of the restaurant as we finish our cookies. We head toward the parking lot, though we left the car parked on Shattuck Avenue and I know that Levi bikes everywhere.

"Where are we going?" I really, really want alone time with Levi, but I don't know how to get rid of Matt and Oscar.

"I'm kind of tired," Matt says.

"Come on, it's only eight p.m.," Oscar says, although it's

closer to nine. "We can't just sit in the hotel."

The three of us look at Levi, Berkeley resident and default tour guide. Levi smiles. "Sorry, guys, but I only made plans for Ethan and me."

Did I mention he was perfect?

OSCAR

Matt and I walk along Telegraph Avenue looking for something to do. Not much is open this late. And it's winter break, so there aren't even any hot college women around. I can't be mad at Ethan for taking off with Levi—it was the reason he agreed to the road trip—but now that means I'm alone with Matt.

But Levi said if we head toward People's Park, there are cool things around there, including a record store where I could find some decent vinyl. Not the most exciting night out, but at least we're *moving*, not stuck in the hotel room where I'd have to pretend to be asleep, and that shit's exhausting.

At least we *were* moving. Matt has stopped in front of a bookstore with a big-ass red-and-white striped awning with Moe's written across it. I have zero interest in the bookstore.

Oh, hell no.

He better not do it.

He does.

He goes inside the bookstore.

Shit.

MATT

"You read? I thought you only watched movies." Oscar shuffles in, looking around the bookstore. I'm looking around, too, at the piles of books next to the register, then downstairs with the wooden bookcases jammed with more books, and up to the tiled stairs that lead to even more books. It's a meet-cute setting, something from a Nineties rom-com starring Meg Ryan.

"I read," I say, perusing the titles of the new arrivals. The store is almost empty except for us and the bored cashier reading *The Collected Poetry of William Carlos Williams*. "Do you read?"

"Do comic books count?"

"I suppose."

Oscar laughs. "Don't go all reading snob on me. All the big blockbuster movies are based on comics, amirite?"

"You really want to discuss the merits of franchise film-making?"

"That'd be a no."

It's taken me awhile, but I've learned that if I call Oscar out on his bluff, he'll back down. It's the opposite with Ethan. He thinks he has something to prove. Oscar's always looking for the path of least resistance.

I spot a display with paperbacks. Aunt Elena's last book is among them. *The Weight of the World: What Society Is Leaving for the Next Generation* by Dr. Elena Vargas.

"I didn't know Aunt Elena had a doctorate. I thought she was still teaching special ed."

"She was until a few years ago," Oscar says. "She thought she'd be taken more seriously if she got a PhD in public policy. She's doing more consulting with politicians these days. She still thinks she can change the world."

"Aunt Elena always sends a copy of her books to my mom, but I guess I haven't really looked at them before." The cover has a graphic of a child's hands holding the world, which is cracking like an egg. I pick it up and flip through the pages. The chapters have titles like "The Lockdown Generation" and "The Post-Traumatic Stress Generation." "My mom says Aunt Elena was always an overachiever."

Oscar makes a face like I said something wrong. He turns to the cashier and calls out, "Where are the graphic novels?"

"Third floor," the cashier says without looking up from William Carlos Williams.

Oscar hits the button for the elevator. I put the book back and follow him.

Up on the third floor, Oscar scans the graphic novels and grabs a volume of *The Walking Dead*.

"Imma catch up on some zombie apocalypse. Lemme know when you're ready to go." He sits down on the floor and starts reading.

I don't know what to do now. I look around the rest of the third floor. It's nonfiction, from anthropology to Zen. Books about Shakespeare have their own area. So do books about tattoos. I'm not seeing any books about films here, though.

I sit on the floor next to Oscar and read the spines of the graphic novels on the shelf. I've seen most of the ones that were made into movies, but there are plenty of titles I've never heard of. I lean back against the bookcase.

"Bro, why'd you come in here if you're not going to read?" Oscar peers at me over the edge of the graphic novel he's holding.

"I like bookstores. And libraries. They're restful."

"Restful," he repeats softly, as though it's a word he's never heard before and is trying it out. He goes back to reading.

I should probably find the film books. I get to my feet.

"You know," Oscar says, still looking down at the book's pages, "we could go *do* something."

"Like what?"

"Like go across the Bay."

"You mean to San Francisco?"

Oscar finally looks up from the graphic novel. His right eyebrow is arched in an exact Leonard Nimoy-Spock imitation. I don't know if he means do a specific impression or he's being facially sarcastic.

"You've never been, right?"

I nod.

"Anything you'd want to see?"

"Actually, there is. But I don't think you'd want to go."

Oscar puts the graphic novel down. He's interested now. "Why?"

"Because someone got shot there."

ETHAN

"That's the student center to the left," Levi says. "The Cesar Chavez Student Center because, you know, Berkeley. And, finally, here's what I wanted you to see."

We stand in the middle of Sproul Plaza, at the entrance of the UC Berkeley campus. Before us is a ginormous gate—or is it an arch?—lit up like a Christmas tree with blue-and-gold twinkle lights. Because, you know, Berkeley.

"It's Sather Gate," Levi says, which at least answers that question. "This is my favorite place to hang out between classes or when I'm stressed out. Come on, there's a bench by the trees."

We walk a few feet to the wooden bench, and I get a better look at the gate once we sit down. Globes of light top four granite columns that span the brick walkway. In the middle, a massive ornate arch with a green patina creates the main gate. The two smaller gates on either side seem like doggie doors next to it.

"It looks like something from a portal fantasy novel," I say, instantly regretting it. *Portal fantasy novel* . . . who knows stuff like that except complete geeks?

Levi nods. "Yeah, I always think Fillory should be on the

other side instead of having to sit through another lecture. Reality is so boring."

Then I remember that this is Levi and he gets my geek appeal. But I can barely concentrate on what he's saying. His arm is stretched across the back of the bench, and his hand lightly brushes against my shoulder. Was that an accident? Is he making a move? I'm suddenly too hot in my coat. Oh, please, please, let him be making a move.

"You should see the place during the day, when school's in session," Levi says. "This is where everyone comes to demonstrate, pro-this and anti-that, handing out leaflets and shouting at people."

"Because, you know, Berkeley," I say.

Levi laughs softly. "Yeah, I guess so."

I lean over and kiss him.

Oh crap, I cannot believe I did that!

Before I can apologize or hyperventilate or die, I realize he is kissing me back.

OSCAR

I don't know why I agreed to this. We've been walking around San Francisco for half an hour, and I still don't know where we're going. We're north of Union Square, past the high-end hotels and in a sketchy neighborhood. But I told Matt I didn't have to know where we were going, as long as we were *going*, so I can't ask now.

Matt doesn't seem confident we're heading in the right direction. He's commandeered my phone to check Google Maps. He keeps walking up Bush Street, and I keep following him. Jesus, I'm winded. Too many damn hills, San Francisco. Ease up on the fog, too. Stop being such a stereotype.

Finally, Matt stops at an alley behind a liquor store. He looks around for a sec, then points at the wall, all excited. "This is it!"

I take my time catching up to him because I don't want him to think I give a shit. I look at the wall. There's a bronze plaque.

> ON APPROXIMATELY THIS SPOT
> MILES ARCHER, PARTNER OF SAM SPADE,
> WAS DONE IN BY BRIGID O'SHAUGHNESSY.

"This is what you wanted to see?" I look from the plaque to Matt. He's smiling like someone gave him a puppy.

"It seemed fitting since falcons are a motif I've been working on," he says.

"What exactly is this?"

"Miles Archer . . . Sam Spade . . . ?" Matt looks at me like he expects me to know the answer. I shrug because it's all I can give him.

"*The Maltese Falcon.* 1941. Humphrey Bogart plays Sam Spade, a private detective. Mary Astor plays Brigid O'Shaughnessy, the femme fatale. She shoots Spade's partner here, but she's off-camera. The audience doesn't find out until later. Sorry for the spoiler."

I shake my head. I am wet and cold and tired. I dig my hands deeper into the pockets of my hoodie. I was pretty wasted when I packed, and it's the warmest thing I have. Matt's coat makes him look a lumberjack, but I bet he's not cold.

"Are you mad?" Matt asks.

I sigh. This guy is wearing me out. "No, we're good."

"I thought it'd be okay because the—you know—shooting—wasn't a real one."

"Then why bother?" I default to asshole.

Matt talks so fast he says in almost one breath, "Because it's an inciting incident. It's what makes the rest of the story happen. It draws the audience in and sets the stakes. It makes people care enough that they put up a plaque to feel like they're part of the story. That's why."

It's a verbal slam dunk I have no comeback for. He lives for this shit. And me, I got nothing.

ETHAN

I open the door to the hotel room, and Levi follows me inside. My brain is still screaming, *This is not happening!*

"When are the cousins coming back?"

"Don't know."

The kissing at Sather Gate still has my heart racing. Levi's lips were as delicious as I thought they would be. Heading to the hotel seemed like the logical next step. How often do two teenagers have easy access to an empty hotel room?

But now the awkwardness and shyness are setting in. We're both standing near the door, not looking at each other or either of the beds.

"Have you ever . . . ?" Levi asks. He doesn't have to say more than that.

"I fooled around a little last year with a guy at music camp who thought he might be bi, but that's it."

Levi shifts his weight from one foot to another. "I haven't either, really."

I try to hide my surprise. "I thought everyone in college just starts hooking up."

"Is that what this is to you? A hookup?" Levi sounds upset.

"No! Levi, you have no idea how much I wanted to meet you because I felt like I already knew you. Like maybe we could be . . ." I trail off pathetically. I am spilling my guts, and I'll scare him off for sure.

"What?" He doesn't sound upset anymore. He sounds hopeful.

I take a deep breath and decide to tell him the truth. "Like maybe we could be more than friends."

"Like maybe I could be your boyfriend?" He's smiling now.

"Yeah, that." I'm smiling, too.

"Like maybe I thought the same thing."

"Like maybe we're a couple now?"

He takes my hand. "Like maybe so."

I look at his hand in mine. It feels right. It feels perfect.

Levi pulls me in for a kiss. "Show me what you learned at music camp."

MATT

The train is almost empty as we head back to Berkeley. I sit by the door while Oscar slouches in a seat a couple of rows away. His eyes are closed, but I don't think he's asleep.

He's told me repeatedly that he doesn't mind that I dragged him to the spot where Miles Archer got shot. He even insisted that I use his phone to take a selfie with the plaque.

But I still think it was selfish of me to take him there. We could have gone to one of the streets where the chase scene in *Bullitt* was filmed or to the *Mrs. Doubtfire* house. But those were only locations. They weren't important as plot points. Dashiell Hammett stood in that alley and thought, *This is where Miles dies. This is what sets everything in motion.*

I have to be sure I wasn't being selfish. I move to the seat next to Oscar.

"Whaddup, cuz?" He still doesn't open his eyes.

"I sorry, I just want to make sure—"

His eyes pop open. "Stop apologizing, 'kay? I get it. Movies are your thing. That was important to you. I'm the one who said let's go to San Francisco. I don't have to be as into it as you. Fake people getting shot is better than real people getting shot. At first I thought you wanted to go where that Harvey Milk dude was killed, because I know that was a movie, too. *The Maltese Falcon* thing at least has real movie geek cred. We're solid, bro."

I decide he's being honest with me and it really is okay. But he's said something that has me curious.

"What is your thing?"

Oscar blinks. "What?"

"You said movies are my thing. What's yours?" He could tell me to eff off, but there has to be something besides recreational drug use that has meaning for him.

Oscar shifts in his seat and looks out into the blackness of the subway tunnel. The way his face is reflected back in the window, his hoodie hiding his eyes in shadows, is a close-up of pure loneliness.

"Baseball. It used to be baseball."

"Why used to be?"

Oscar continues to look out the window rather than at me. But he doesn't tell me to eff off. "I played first base in Little League. I was a good runner, too, stole a lot of bases. So I'm in fifth grade, we're playing baseball during PE, and I see the principal, the vice principal, and two cops approach the coach. And I'm like, what did Coach do? I was afraid he was a child molester or something, and they were going to arrest him. I liked Coach Schuler. He was a bit of a hard-ass but basically fair and really loved the game.

"I loved baseball, too. I got that from my dad. He knew all the stats, and we went to Cactus League games during spring training. We even planned on going to every Major League Baseball stadium, just me and him.

"But instead of that bright, shining future, I see all these adults heading toward me. And I'm like, damn, what did *I* do? I'd set off a few illegal fireworks with a couple of friends the day before. Thought maybe it started a wildfire, and they were able to trace it back to us. But Ryan and Liam were on the field, too, and the cops weren't coming toward them.

"Finally, the principal and the cops have me surrounded, and the principal asks me to come with him to his office. And I'm like, no way, José, I want to know what the hell is going on. I see that teachers are on the field, rounding up the kids, telling them the school's in lockdown. All the adults looked so serious, scared even, and I found myself between the two cops, who were hustling me toward the principal's office. And then the principal told me there's a gunman at the high school, holding my dad's classroom hostage.

"I don't know what he said after that. Everything was a blur for the next, oh, three or four years. I couldn't play baseball anymore. Couldn't even watch it on TV. Threw out all my jerseys, all my equipment. I was done. Everything good in my life ended that day."

The subway car screeches to a halt. It's our stop, and as the doors open, Oscar bolts for them. But I block his way. I have to say something.

"I didn't know." I wish it were something better than that.

"You never will." He slips past me and exits the train.

ETHAN

Me:
I met Levi!

Jiwon:
YAY!

Me:
I kissed Levi!

Jiwon:
😍

Me:
😇

Jiwon:
🤣

Me:
We are officially a couple!

Jiwon:

Your grandma is dancing in heaven.

Me:
He's everything I hoped for, only better.

Jiwon:

And . . . ?

Me:

We decided to take the physical stuff slow.

But kissing was definitely involved.

Jiwon:

Me:

I still can't believe it happened.

Everything was 💯 .

Jiwon:

I knew he was the one for you, E!

You nerds deserve each other.

Me:

G2G.

OSCAR

Ethan is texting when Matt and I enter the hotel room. Big surprise. He's sprawled out on one of the beds and puts his phone next to him when he sees us come in.

I plop down face first on the other bed. I know I promised to sleep in the chair, but I am fucking exhausted. Let Matt decide where he's going to sleep tonight. He's been quiet since we left the BART station. Because what can he say after what I said to him? This is why I don't talk to people.

Matt got to me with his question because he asked about *me*. No one does that. Not even the therapists. They ask about my feelings, the very thing I'm trying not to have. But Matt wore me down with his sincerity. He actually believes that I could give a shit about something.

So I told him the truth. The life I used to have. The life that doesn't seem real anymore. What a loser I am to spill my guts like that. At least I didn't completely wimp out and show him the letter.

I've said sorry so many times.

I'm jonesing to get baked, but I've been a dick for not doing my share of the driving. I should probably stay sober for the next few days.

"Hey," I say, interrupting Matt and Ethan's conversation about who the hell knows. "I'll drive the first leg tomorrow morning."

"'Kaaaaay." Ethan stretches the word out like a piece of gum, not really sure what to do with it now that it's out.

I roll over onto my back and see Ethan's still sprawled out and Matt's sitting cross-legged on the corner of the bed. I realize that whatever conversation they were having included me, and I responded with something completely random. I am a master at reading WTF looks between people.

"Where's your boyfriend?" I ask.

Ethan breaks into a smile. The question does the trick and gets the convo away from me. "Levi went home, but he's promised to meet us for breakfast before we leave."

"You guys a couple now?" I ask.

His smile gets wider. "Yes!"

"Even with the long-distance thing? Even though he's older?"

"He's only a year older. And the distance thing we'll figure out."

"Must be nice." It sounds sarcastic once it's out of my mouth, but I'm serious. It must be nice to have someone give a shit about you.

Matt gets a weird look on his face. "Was Levi here? In the hotel room?"

"Well, duh," says Ethan.

"I'm not comfortable with that," Matt says.

"Let me get into my time machine and fix that for you." Ethan sits up. The two of them are in a face-off on either side of the bed.

"It's none of our business what Ethan did," I say.

"Or didn't do," Ethan says. "Gay is not synonymous with promiscuous."

"I didn't say that," Matt says.

"Then what exactly is your problem?" Ethan asks.

"The Old Testament condemns homosexuality. How can you—"

"Can we not do this now?" I ask. "It's fucking late and we have to get up early."

"No, I've got this," Ethan says. "Levi and I are Reform Jews. We have a more progressive interpretation of the Torah because we look at the moral message of the entire Torah. And that message is simply to love each other, which is so much better than obsessing over a few verses. You Christian fundamentalists believe every word of the Bible is literally true, but it doesn't have to be literally true to be spiritually true. Believing God is inclusive makes more sense than believing he's homophobic."

"I'm trying to understand your point of view," Matt says, "but that doesn't mean I have to agree with it."

"Ditto," Ethan says. His phone pings and he looks down at it. He laughs softly and types something. He's forgotten we're even here.

I lug myself off the bed and head for the john. But first I stop in front of Matt. "All that stuff I said earlier? Just a bunch of bullshit. Like everything else I say."

Matt tilts his head like a curious spaniel. "If you say so."

I'm not sure if that's supposed to be a joke or not. If it is, it's a good one. I laugh as I go to take a piss.

DECEMBER 31

MATT

Ethan has been kicking me all night in his sleep, so I'm awake when my phone rings. I jump out of bed and dive for my coat hanging over the chair. I dig my phone out of the coat pocket before it can ring a second time.

"Hey, Mom," I whisper as I walk into the bathroom and shut the door. I knew it was Mom before I looked at the number. No one else would call me before 7 a.m.

"I didn't wake you, did I? I thought you boys would be getting an early start."

"We were sleeping in a little—"

"Oh, *mijo*, I'll—"

"Don't worry about it, Mom. It's fine." I catch a glance of myself in the mirror over the sink. The dark circles under my eyes. The morning stubble along my jaw. I stick my tongue out at the mirror and see white film on top of it. I didn't even floss my teeth last night because I was so exhausted.

"Good, because I didn't want to disturb you. I was getting worried because you didn't call yesterday."

Another thing I forgot to do. I had been planning on calling her after dinner, but then we ended up going to San Francisco.

"Sorry." It's the only thing I can tell her that's true. She still thinks we took the route Dad planned for us. We're supposed to be somewhere in Utah right now.

"How are things going?"

It's another thing I can't honestly answer, but this time because I have no idea what the answer is. How *is* it going?

"The car's been working fine." Not a lie.

"And your cousins? How are they?"

I remember that I said I'd witness to them about Christ as part of the bargain to be able to go. I have not witnessed to them.

"They're fine, too." I search my brain for something else to add. "Ethan is a very cautious driver."

I hear Mom stifle a chuckle. "That's good to hear. Do you think you'll beat the snowstorm headed for Provo?"

"We'll probably miss it." A lie of omission is still a lie.

"I have news. Your aunties and I have agreed on what to do with the restaurant."

"Are you selling?" I ask.

"Remember Carlos, the manager? We're going into a partnership with him and keeping the restaurant in Portland open. And I may have other big news soon."

"Okay." I have nothing else to say. "Hey, Mom, I've got to go. I will call you later, I promise."

"You better, mister. Love you. Happy New Year!"

I have completely forgotten it's New Year's Eve today.

"I love you, too. Happy New Year."

ETHAN

Matt's making a lot of noise for someone not trying to make any noise. I roll over to look at him, even though he's a fuzzy lump since I don't have my contacts in.

"Whattimeisit?" It's a slur of words because I am still half-asleep and I can't get my mouth to work right.

"Almost seven thirty."

"Crap." That wakes me up. "I told Levi we'd meet him for breakfast at eight."

I write Levi a quick text that we'll be at Saul's Deli around eight-ish. I debate whether or not I should add *XOXO* at the end of it. I want to show affection, but maybe that's too much this early in our relationship. Everything last night was so perfect, and I don't want ruin it. Are hugs and kisses first thing in the morning playful or needy? Since we've moved from flirting to being a couple, I have no idea what I'm doing.

I put my glasses on and see that Matt is packing. He's already showered and shaved. Oscar's still asleep, his hands curled in fists under his chin. His eyelashes are long and dark against his cheek, the kind that Jiwon says aren't fair on boys when she has to struggle with eyelash curlers and mascara.

These two would be no help with relationship questions. I'm not even sure if Matt is allowed to be alone with a girl. And Oscar may have plenty of experience, but not with relationships.

Jiwon wouldn't be awake yet, and even if she were, she'd be no help, either. She promised her parents not to date until college in exchange for a trip across Europe as a graduation present.

So I'm on my own here, relationship-wise. I decide on a winky face emoji. Levi immediately sends a text back with a winky kissy face. Maybe I don't have to worry about looking too needy. Maybe he actually needs me.

The thought makes me warm and toasty and gooey inside, like a Pop-Tart. Today is going to be a good day.

I pull aside the curtains to let in the morning light. Except it's overcast and gray outside. Doesn't matter. My inner Pop-Tart will not be denied.

"Time to wake up, sunshine!" I say to Oscar. "I've got some angry antiestablishment rock for you!" I put my phone by his head and hit play. Rick Astley's "Never Gonna Give You Up" blasts from the speaker.

"Are you seriously rickrolling me?" Oscar mumbles as he rubs his eyes. "Stop with the Eighties already!"

I laugh as I dance around the room. "Never!"

OSCAR

I'm on my third cup of coffee, even though I got maybe six hours of sleep, the most I've gotten in days. Actual dead-tired sleep. I might have even dreamed. I might have even dreamed about a freshly cut field and the smell of oil on a new glove. I might have even dreamed I was happy.

But that's all gone now.

Ethan and Levi are annoying the hell out of me. They're finishing each other's sentences and laughing and eating each other's food. "Hey, cuz," I say before I hear for the millionth time how damn happy they are, "we gotta hit the road." I tap an imaginary watch on my wrist.

Matt says the first thing he's said in the past hour. "Yeah."

Ethan and Levi sigh in unison. That makes them laugh their asses off like the idiots in love they are.

My eye roll is so epic it may give me an aneurysm. "Imma get the check, then we're outta here."

Ethan and Levi sigh again. This time they don't laugh.

ETHAN

I'm going to cry and I don't want to do that. I hear Oscar's constant honking of the car horn, and it's making me mad. I don't need a reminder that he's taking me away from Levi.

Levi. I thought he was perfect yesterday. And yet he's even more perfect today. Didn't Grandma Lupe just die? Am I allowed to be this happy?

Oscar lays on the horn again.

"Goddamn it, Oscar, give me a minute!" I shout.

I see Matt wince at my blasphemy as he adjusts his seat belt in the passenger seat of the Beast.

Levi flashes Oscar a peace sign. He hasn't let go of my hand the whole time we've stood outside of the deli. I don't want to be the first to let go.

But I do.

"So . . ." I stop, afraid that I will break down if I say anything more. The reality is setting in that I don't know when I'll see Levi again.

He wraps me in a hug. "Don't say good-bye, okay? Good-byes suck."

"Happy New Year?" I say.

"Happy New Year."

We kiss. But not good-bye. We kiss in the New Year.

MATT

I was worried about Oscar's driving, but he's a confident, albeit fast, driver. He's found a classic rock station on the radio and tries to get us to sing along to "Bohemian Rhapsody."

"Come on, Matty, it's a classic. There's even a movie about it," Oscar says.

"I've seen the movie, but that doesn't mean I know the words to the song."

"Ethan? Where's the love for Queen? Freddie Mercury? Total gay icon."

"I had to play a symphony orchestration of 'Bohemian Rhapsody' for our winter concert. Too soon to want to ever hear the song again. And don't get me started on heteros' appropriation of gay icons."

"Doesn't the song disturb you?" I don't know why Oscar wants to sing it. It's about a man who shoots someone and gets the death penalty.

"Twisted, right?" Oscar sings along to the high falsetto part before it breaks into hard rock. He bangs his head along to the beat. When he sings the lines that say nothing really matters, I think that's the closest explanation I'll get to why he likes it.

Another song comes on. I recognize it from old *CSI* episodes. Oscar pumps his fist. "Yes! The Who!"

We've passed a town called Hayward on the 580, a backdrop of brown hills and gray skies for miles. I wish I had inspiration for another scene, maybe something that could tie in the falcon motif. But nothing's coming to mind. I could, I suppose, talk to my cousins. I did promise my parents I'd witness to them. I have to find the right approach, though, or they'll laugh. Or worse, they'll shut me down completely.

How do I tell Oscar that God loves him, that God has a plan for him? That his pain and suffering is nothing compared to what Jesus did for him on the cross? A relationship with Christ would give him the hope and healing he needs. It'd probably be easier to convert Ethan than to get Oscar to see how Christ could change his life.

I pray for guidance on what to say.

OSCAR

I can't get anyone to sing some tunes with me, which is no surprise. Ethan is sulking about Levi, and Matt's all quiet. I can't get a read on Matt. Sometimes he's so damn literal and other times he's observant as fuck.

"When we get to LA, what do you guys want to do first?" I ask.

"I've been there a million times," Ethan says. "My other grandma lives in Newport Beach."

"Yeah, but it's New Year's Eve. If we're lucky, we'll get there in time to celebrate."

Ethan sighs. "I suppose."

"Dude, do not be a downer for the rest of the trip because your boyfriend isn't around. It's what you signed up for when you decided to do the long-distance thing."

"Thank you, Oscar, for pointing out the obvious. Also, fuck you." Ethan opens the tin of sugar cookies. "I'm finishing off the rest of Mrs. Kaminsky's Christmas cookies."

"Matty, besides 'SC, what's on the bucket list? The Hollywood sign? Universal Studios? Sunset Strip?"

"Can we go to the beach?" Ethan asks. "I want to stick my feet in the ocean."

"Oh, now he has an opinion. Let Matty choose. But personally, I hope it's not a cemetery to visit a dead celebrity. Not my idea of ringing in the New Year, you know?"

Jesus, I should have laid off the coffee. How many cups did I have? I'm more buzzy than after taking an Adderall.

"Before we decide where to go, I want you to know that I won't be doing any drinking or drugs or anything like that, so I guess that makes me the designated driver," says Matt.

"Cool, cool. Thanks for being the responsible one. But I promised you guys last night I'd lay off the self-medicating." I'm not offended he didn't believe me when I made that promise. I may have not meant it when I said it. But now I feel on the hook to deliver.

"Oscar, my mom just sent me a text," Ethan says. "She wants to know what you want of Grandma's. She says your mom asked you, but you hadn't decided."

That's one way to put it. I ignored the text Mom sent this morning asking the same thing.

"Uh . . . I'm still deciding."

"I'm getting Grandpa Manny's watch," Ethan says. "It's a 1970s Rado Companion. Grandma wore it every day after he died. She said wearing his watch felt like time couldn't separate them. Grandpa had his faults, but Grandma really loved him."

"I didn't know she was that sentimental," Matt says.

"Hey, why weren't you guys ever at Thanksgiving at the restaurant?" Ethan asks.

"We usually spent Christmas at Grandma's instead of

Thanksgiving," Matt says. "Except for the past few years. My dad hasn't been able to travel much."

"We visited Portland for Thanksgiving a couple of times," I say. "When I was little. Then after my dad died, we always did the holidays with his family in Tucson."

"Oh," Ethan says quietly.

Nothing ends a conversation faster than mentioning my dead dad.

"You were at Thanksgiving once when I was there," I say. "We were about five or six. You were crying because your dad wouldn't let you drink his beer."

Ethan makes a puffing noise of disbelief. "That didn't— HOLY SHIT!"

ETHAN

This fog wasn't here a minute ago.

That semitruck wasn't here a second ago.

I just met Levi. I can't die now!

Oscar hits the brakes until they're screeching like the Nazgûl.

Maybe it's my own screaming that I hear.

I DO NOT WANT TO FUCKING DIE!

MATT

Everything stops.

I open my eyes.

We're halfway in the lane and half on the shoulder. There's about ten inches between us and the back of an eighteen-wheeler.

"Thank you, Jesus," I say softly.

"Shit, yeah," Oscar says. "Thank you, Jesus Christ Almighty!" He raises his hands like he's at a prayer meeting. I'm not sure if that's meant to be blasphemous or if Oscar truly means it. I'm not going to try to figure out how this is part of God's plan, but it must be. Somehow.

"Yay, we didn't die!" Ethan moves in for a fist bump with me and then with Oscar. "Now what?"

The fog has gotten thicker. I can barely see more than a few yards ahead of us. "Are the fog lights on?" I ask.

"Uhhhh . . ." Oscar looks around the dashboard. I point to the controls on the steering column. He flips the fog lights on. They don't help much.

"I don't think we're going anywhere for a while," Ethan says, looking at his phone. "There's a bad accident about a mile ahead. Looks like it's backed up."

"I can at least get the Beast back on the road." Oscar inches the car over until we're off the shoulder.

Dad was right. Fog on the I-5 is to be expected. I was negligent for not checking the weather report. I didn't even instruct Oscar on where the proper lights were. "This is my fault. I should have known better."

"Dude, no," Oscar says at the same time Ethan says, "Don't be ridiculous."

"But it is. The Beast is my car and my responsibility. You're my passengers and you're my responsibility, too."

"Don't be so hard on yourself, Matty," Oscar says. "I'm the one driving, you guys are my responsibility when I'm behind the wheel. I was clowning on Ethan, not paying attention, and I lost control of the car. My fault, end of story."

"As much as I'd love to play pin-the-blame-on-Oscar," Ethan says, "it's no one's fault. Except maybe the fog's."

I shake my head. They're being nice, but they're wrong. I know my duty. I promised my parents I'd witness to my cousins and I've been avoiding it. Avoiding it right until the point we almost died. *This* is God's plan. I will not have a better time than now to tell them about God's word.

OSCAR

Matt launches into his Jesus-Died-for-Your-Sins sermon, and I'm thinking about this girl from tenth grade, Kayla Acosta, who tried to save me. Other girls had tried to "save me," girls who thought if they loved me enough, I would learn to love myself (as Dr. Bergstrom theorized during our sessions). I'd manage to get a blow job or two out of them, but they eventually realized what an asshole I am and that no, their love would not be enough to save me.

Kayla was different. We were partners for a social studies project on food from other countries. She wanted to do gummy bears, which were her favorite food. Thanks, Germany, for the whimsically shaped empty calories. She pushed me to do my share of the work. I actually did it. We got an A.

She wasn't one of the popular girls, but she knew everyone and everyone liked her. She was four foot ten with shiny black hair that reached her butt. She was Filipino, I think. Maybe Guatemalan. I never asked. People did ask her, though. Where you from? Mesa, she'd say.

Kayla didn't pity me. She didn't romanticize me. She didn't

act like I was some kind of celebrity because I'd been on TV. She would catch sight of me in the hallway between classes and look happy to see me. She'd sit by me on the bus and talk about whatever was on her mind, not expecting me to reply, but expecting me to listen. She was, for lack of a better word, my friend.

I needed to know why was she so kind to me. How was it when she smiled at me, I knew she was actually looking at *me* and not at the kid whose dad had been killed in a school shooting? Not even teachers or Dr. Bergstrom had been able to pull that one off.

One day, while we were riding the bus home, I asked her.

She smiled at me and—no joke—her smile was a thing of beauty and wonder. She put her hand on my arm. "Oh, Oscar, I'm kind because Jesus was kind. Every day, I want to shine my light through Him and for Him."

I jerked my arm away from her. "Now you're going to tell me Jesus died for my sins and if I accept him as my personal savior, I'll go to heaven, right? Because anyone who doesn't is going to hell. So my dad, who was Catholic, went to hell because he never said the 'Sinner's Prayer.'" I used air quotes aggressively. "And even though he killed my dad, Tanner Aaron Gibbs is going to heaven because he says he accepted Jesus as his personal savior while he was awaiting trial. Because that makes perfect sense."

Kayla smiled, but for once, it was forced. "Oscar, I'm sorry somebody said that to you. I don't know God's plan, but I believe there's a reason for everything."

"There might be a reason, but that doesn't mean it's a good one."

"I want to believe there is. I want to believe that there's a power greater than me. It makes me feel special that Jesus gives so much without asking for anything in return, except our thanks."

"I have NOTHING to thank him for."

Kayla stopped smiling. In fact, she was blinking back tears. "I'm not explaining myself very well, am I? But I think it comes down to our free will to choose to believe in Him. That's where faith comes in, that we believe this choice makes a difference in our lives. If believing in Jesus helps me be a better person, then I'm going to believe in Jesus."

"Can't you be a good person without Jesus?"

"Probably. But if it makes it easier for me be a good person because I believe that He helps me through the hard parts, and it makes me happy to do what I do, then why shouldn't I believe in Him?"

"Because if God exists, he's a scam artist. He wants your love and obedience and then takes everything away from you. Why? To get you to turn to him when he's the one who screwed you over in the first place? Hate to break it to you, Kayla, but there's no one there to help you through the hard parts."

Kayla put her hand on my arm again, this time giving it a squeeze, like she wanted to give me a hug but wasn't sure if she should.

I really wanted her to give me a hug.

"You may not believe in God, Oscar, but you have to believe in yourself. And if you can't believe in yourself, Jesus believes in you and I believe in you. I pray for you because I see the sadness in you. I pray that the sadness doesn't become hopelessness."

My face became hot. It was like she knew all my secrets. I didn't know what to say. So I said the worst thing possible. "Fuck you, Kayla. Fuck you and your holier-than-thou bullshit."

We reached her stop. Other kids were piling out of the bus, but Kayla took a moment to give her head a little shake. I could still see the tears in her eyes, though. "God bless you, Oscar."

And she was gone.

I haven't spoken to Kayla since then because I got expelled the following day for smoking pot in the boys' locker room. After that, Mom sent me to St. Catherine's Academy.

As Matt goes on and on, I nod and pretend to listen, but I just wish I hadn't been such a dick to Kayla.

ETHAN

I don't know if I should feel insulted or relieved that Matt's not trying that hard to convert me. He's focusing on Oscar, barely even looking back at me.

Oscar seems into what Matt's saying, nodding a lot and making agreeing noises. If Oscar wants to clean up and start fresh, maybe the Jesus thing isn't a bad way to go.

"Yeah, I get what you're saying," Oscar interrupts Matt. "But why are so many Christians assholes? Like about gays and who gets to go into what bathroom and freaking out if a woman makes a decision about her own body?"

"Yeah," I say, resting my chin on the corner of Oscar's headrest. "I'd like to know that, too."

"Not all Christians are like that," Matt says, super defensive.

"But plenty of them are and not enough people call them on it," Oscar says. "Didn't Jesus go all apeshit on the moneylenders in the temple, ripping them a new one because of their hypocrisy? That's the kind of thing Christians need to do to get people to stop thinking they're assholes. It's like what Ethan said about obsessing over a few Bible verses and ignoring the main message. I mean—and, Ethan, correct me if I'm wrong—but Leviticus is where it says not to eat pork. And I bet these Christians love them some bacon and pork chops and chorizo and all the delicious things that come from little piggies."

"Yep," I say, "no pigs, no shrimp, no shellfish in general, can't mix meat and milk products, so cheeseburgers and sausage pizza are out."

"Leviticus is Old Testament," Matt says, "but Jesus brings in a new covenant with His resurrection."

"Pigs become legit, but gays still aren't? Doesn't compute, bro," Oscar says. "If Jesus brings in a—whaddaya call it—new covenant, Mr. SAT Words, I'm pretty sure I remember enough of Sunday school that it's supposed to be 'Do unto others as you'd have them do unto you' and all that Golden Rule shit. My question still stands . . . why are so many Christians assholes?"

I am both delighted and offended by what Oscar's said. It's harsh but also kind of true. I'm curious to know how Matt responds.

"I know there are plenty of people who call themselves Christians, but who don't really walk on the road of righteousness," Matt says. "God knows their hearts and they'll have to answer for it on Judgment Day."

"They shouldn't get a free ride on their jacked-up Christianity until Judgment Day," Oscar says. "And don't deny you were freaked out when you found out Ethan was gay, and you gave him a hard time about his boyfriend being in our hotel room."

Matt looks down at his hands, the fingers interlocked as through he's praying. "I want to reflect the spirit of Christ in what I do, but I'm human enough to make mistakes." He makes eye contact with me. "I want to know more about your faith so I can understand you better."

"Is that you apologizing?" I ask. Matt seems sincere, but he actually hasn't said the words *I'm sorry*.

He nods. "I'm sorry if I offended you."

Okay, it's a conditional apology, but there's a big goofy grin on my face. There have been microaggressions and not-so-microaggressions since I've come out, and this is the first time I've gotten something resembling an acknowledgment of regret. It still feels incredible.

"I accept your apology. And as a Reform Jew, we don't really believe in Judgment Day. We also don't believe in heaven and hell. Not like Christian heaven or hell. What we have are the High Holidays, when we reflect on our actions during the past year and atone for any wrongs. You do mitzvahs—good deeds—because helping people is what you do. You do what you can to make the world better and that's your reward. Now Jiwon, she's Baptist and was raised fundie like you, Matt. But now she's so over it. She doesn't like how smug and cliquish people from her church can be. They're super judgey about everything she does because it might be 'worldly.' She's not even supposed to wear mascara. She started going to an Episcopal church because they're progressive about gays and women's rights and stuff like that."

"That's what I'm talking about," Oscar says. "God's gotta be bigger than those conservative shitheads let him be."

Just then, the fog lifts.

"Oh fuck," I say in a whisper.

MATT

EXT. HIGHWAY — DAY

A heavy fog blankets the highway. PAN ACROSS
a silhouette of cars creeping along in
traffic. Behind an eighteen-wheeler is a
burgundy 1988 Ford Thunderbird.

A POLICE OFFICER in a yellow slicker directs
cars to follow a line of orange cones.

As the Thunderbird passes the first cone,
the fog lifts enough to give visibility to
a MASSIVE CAR PILEUP. There's a chaos of
police cars, ambulances, fire trucks, and
tow trucks nearby.

People involved in the accident are in
shock, bloodied, sitting on the ground or
in the back of emergency vehicles. Some are

on phones, some are crying, some are cuddled
together under silver thermal blankets.

The Thunderbird continues to creep along
past the accident and the orange cones.

TWO PARAMEDICS lift up a gurney with a body
bag and take it to the nearest ambulance.

> BACK SEAT PASSENGER (O.S.)
> Is that a body bag?

A THIRD PARAMEDIC zips a body bag that's on
the ground. Behind her, there are two more
zipped bags on the ground.

POV OF THIRD PARAMEDIC as she glances up and
sees the Thunderbird pass by. She sees the
faces of three young men, their eyes wide.

The Back Seat Passenger puts his hand on
the window, in what might be a wave or a
benediction.

Third Paramedic sighs and goes back to work.

A FALCON flies over the accident and heads
south.

OSCAR

After we pass the accident, traffic clears up and I start to make up time. No one says anything.

My mind's racing, though. If Ethan hadn't lingered all gooey-eyed saying good-bye to Levi, we would have been in the middle of that shit.

The anxiety has kicked in. Fucking PTSD. I'm probably driving faster than I should. My leg is shaking, and if I concentrate on keeping my foot on the pedal, I don't have to think about what we saw.

I wish I could light up right now. I should have paid more attention to the calming techniques Dr. Bergstrom talked about.

After we put in a few miles, Matt's the first to speak up.

"I don't have all the answers, Oscar. Some of those people we saw at the accident might be thanking God or cursing Him right now. But I think the point of faith is that you believe what's true in your heart. For me, that truth is Jesus. My faith gives me strength that I don't think I'd have otherwise."

"Yeah, I've heard that before," I say, thinking of Kayla. Why was I so shitty to the only person who was kind to me? I should have told her I'm sorry years ago.

I'm not asking for forgiveness because I don't deserve it.

My leg starts shaking again. I try to remember how to breathe.

ETHAN

Levi:
What's up?

Me:
Just saw a bad accident.

Levi:
You safe?

Me:
Yeah, but I wish I was with you.

Levi:
Me too.

Me:
So this is what being in a long distance relationship means? Constantly wishing we were together again?

Levi:
But it'll be worth it when we finally do see each other.

Me:
So until then . . . ?

Levi:
We keep each other's spirits up.

Me:

Make me laugh?

Levi:

A challenge! You're on. Knock, knock.

Me:

Who's there?

Levi:

To.

Me:

To who?

Levi:

To whom.

Me:

Grammar nerd.

Levi:

But did it work?

Me:

A little.

Levi:

Bear poops smell unbearable, but clown poops smell funny.

Me:

🤣

Levi:

Bathroom humor FTW!

Me:

Still miss you.

Levi:

Stay strong. 🥰

PART III

LOS ANGELES

OSCAR

Traffic along Hollywood Boulevard is bumper to bumper. We can't go more than a few feet before we're stuck behind a line of cars trying to make a right turn but they can't because of the swarms of pedestrians crossing. If we had somewhere to be, I'd be laying on the horn and flipping the bird like crazy. But we got nowhere to be all night, and the Beast is perfect for going low and slow.

"Turn onto Ivar," Ethan says, looking at directions on his phone.

"Roger that. Now what?"

"Look for a place to park."

"We just passed a lot," I say.

"You didn't see the sign?" Ethan says. "It's fifty bucks!"

"Dude, I'll spot you the fifty." A group of girls in tight skirts and high heels runs across the street right in front of the Beast. Normally, a group of girls in tight skirts and high heels is a welcome sight. Tonight, I blast the horn. They laugh and one of them shouts over her shoulder, "Sorry!"

"There's a spot!" Ethan yells in my ear.

"Where?"

"There!" Ethan sticks his arm out from the back seat and points over my shoulder to an indefinite spot.

"Three cars ahead on the left, past the red Mazda," says Matt.

"Now those are directions," I say, cruising into a three-point turn. The car behind us honks at the Beast. I smile and give the soccer mom in the Lexus SUV a courtesy wave. She doesn't smile back.

"Fucking LA," I mutter as I finish the turn and grab the spot. "She probably thinks we're undocumented."

No one hears me, though, as we get out of the car. The night air is cool, but nowhere near as bad as the freezing fog of San Francisco. There's a vibe in the air, too—excitement mixed with anticipation.

"We okay?" I ask as Ethan checks out the parking sign farther down the street.

"I guess?"

Matt goes to join him while I lock the car. They're still looking at the sign when I catch up to them.

"Well?" I ask.

Ethan shrugs. "You tell me."

I read the sign. Then I realize there are multiple signs.

> **NO PARKING**
> **3 A.M.–5 A.M.**
> **VEHICLES WITH**
> **L5 PERMIT EXEMPT**

2 HOUR PARKING
ONLY
9 A.M.–6 P.M.
EXCEPT SUNDAYS
AND HOLIDAYS
←

NO PARKING
ANY TIME
→

"What the serious fuck?" I say.

"New Year's Eve is a holiday, right?" Ethan asks.

"Are we on the right-side arrow or left-side arrow?" asks Matt.

"We're kind of in the middle," Ethan says.

"Matty, it's your car. What do you want to do?" I ask.

Matt has that wheel-turning look he gets when he's thinking. "I think I'd prefer the parking lot."

"Okay, lot it is," I say.

We all pile into the Beast and head back the way we came.

"What?" Ethan says in disbelief when we see the sign that the lot is full. "We were just here a minute ago."

"Want to look for another lot or go back to the spot on the street?" I ask Matt.

"If it's still there," Ethan says.

"Not helping, Ethan," I say.

Matt takes a deep breath. "Let's try the street again."

MATT

I did not anticipate parking in Hollywood on New Year's Eve would be this difficult. It's painfully obvious now that we're in the middle of it. At least I can trust Oscar to park the Beast. He's done a fine job navigating the traffic and the crowds. Probably better than I would have. The only time there's traffic as bad as this in Santa Fe is during Las Posadas and I avoid it.

"It's still free!" Ethan points to the empty curb from the back seat.

A yellow Mini Cooper approaches from the north, heading for the same spot.

"Oh, no, you don't!" Oscar guns the Beast. Suddenly, we're in a game of chicken. I don't see this ending well.

"Stop the car!" I shout.

Oscar brakes hard. Without thinking, I unbuckle my seat belt with one hand and open the passenger door with other. I race over to the spot as the Mini Cooper is about to pull in. I lay on the ground with my arms and legs spread-eagled so the Mini can't get in without running me over.

The driver rolls down the window. He's a middle-aged white

guy with a beard. "What the hell are you doing? That's my spot!"

"I know you won't believe me," I say, "but technically, we were here first."

"That's a serious dick move," the guy says, turning red. He starts to nudge the car closer to me.

"Just try it, asshole!" Ethan shouts as he films the guy on his phone.

The driver looks like he's considering his options. Knowing that running me over is one of them is not something I'm happy about.

"Fuck you guys," the driver says as he takes off.

I take a deep breath before I stand up and step onto the curb. Oscar makes a leisurely three-point turn into the spot.

"That was awesome!" Ethan taps on his phone as he gets out of the car. "I'm sending the video to Levi."

Oscar wipes gravel off my back. "Welcome to LA."

ETHAN

"How many selfies can one person take?" Oscar asks as I duck-face in front of the pagoda facade of the Chinese Theatre. The place is packed with tourists stepping in the footprints of celebrities immortalized in concrete blocks. "I thought you've been to LA a million times before."

"Okay, I've been to Orange County a million times before. The last time we came to Hollywood, I was probably ten. And we're here to have fun. This is what fun looks like, Oscar."

I take a photo of him giving me the finger.

"This is freaking cool," Matt says, in the closest thing to swearing I've heard out of him. He's been starstruck since we started walking down Hollywood Boulevard. He oohs and aahs at the names that line the street in stars of pink stone and brass, then goes into lengthy detail about their credits and random trivia. He's a walking Internet Movie Database.

I take a photo of Matt standing in the footprints of Samuel L. Jackson.

Oscar digs his hands deeper in his hoodie pockets and grunts. He's been sober for at least twelve hours, and it's starting to show.

"Maybe it's time we grab something to eat," I say. The smell of fried onions coming from the hot dog cart nearby is one of my all-time favorite smells.

"Now that's a plan," Oscar says.

"How about Mel's Drive-In down the street?" Matt says. "The original restaurant was featured in *American Graffiti*."

"Sounds awesome," I say, although I have no idea what *American Graffiti* is.

One of the knockoff character impersonators taking photos with tourists makes the mistake of trying to hug Oscar. This particular character wears an Elmo costume with dirty red fur and a weird smell like the polish I use to clean my violin.

Oscar dodges Skeevy Elmo, but Skeevy Elmo doesn't take the hint and tries again. "Back off, dude." Oscar gives him a slight nudge to get him to move on.

Skeevy Elmo puts his arms wide, like, *Come at me, bro*!

A small crowd has gathered around as if it's a show at a theme park. Exactly what Skeevy Elmo wants. He starts playing to the crowd. He puts up his furry red paws like he's ready to box Oscar.

Oscar shakes his head. He knows he's beat. "Okay, okay," he says. "Let's hug it out."

They hug. The crowd applauds. Skeevy Elmo takes a bow. More applause. I'm laughing so hard, I'm going to pee my pants.

Skeevy Elmo encourages Oscar to take a bow. Oscar smiles and gives Skeevy Elmo the finger. Skeevy Elmo puts his hands on his head and shakes it like, *Oh, no, you didn't*.

The crowd gasps. "There are children here! They shouldn't

have to see something like that!" an overweight blonde woman shouts.

"Then don't bring them to fucking Hollywood," Oscar says.

OSCAR

"What do you mean you don't have video of it? You were filming everything! You even took video of the TMZ tour bus!"

Ethan finishes chewing his meat loaf before he answers me. "It happened so fast, I just didn't, okay? Believe me, I would've loved to have a permanent record of you taking on Skeevy Elmo."

"Skeevy Elmo?" Matt says. "I was thinking of him as Homeless Elmo. What does *skeevy* mean?"

"Something that's gross or nasty," Ethan says.

"Skeevy," Matt repeats, like he's filing it away for later. "That sounds right."

I shake my head in disappointment. "We should have made Matt the official documenter of the trip. He would have gotten video."

"Documentarian," Matt says. "Not documenter."

"Whatever," Ethan says. "It's my phone, so you're stuck with me. And no one told me that we were archiving this trip for posterity."

"No, we can't," Matt says, panicky all of sudden. "My parents still don't know we're in California."

"Dude, chillax. It's not like we're posting anything on social media." I give Ethan a look. "Right?"

"I'm only sending stuff to Levi. And Jiwon. But that's it. There's no way it can get back to your parents."

"See?" I point a soggy chili fry across the table at Matt. "We're cool."

"Hey, are those girls watching us?" Ethan casually tilts his head at a booth near the retro jukebox in this tourist-trap 1950s diner. A white tall blonde with glasses and an olive-skinned brunette with a nose stud are, in fact, looking over at us and whispering to each other.

They realize that they've been caught. Glasses stands up. Nose Stud puts her hand on the other girl's arm to stop her. Glasses says something to Nose Stud. Nose Stud reluctantly stands up.

"They're coming over here," Ethan whispers, all dramatic.

I arch my eyebrow. They're both cute, but Nose Stud is more my type. Glasses is clearly the leader, though, since she reaches our table first.

"You look super familiar. Weren't you on *America's Got Talent*?" she asks me.

"Nope, but I've been on TV." Which is technically true.

"Yeah?" Glasses is suspicious, but she wants to believe she's talking to someone famous.

"Yeah. Done a few commercials. I'm Manuel," I say.

Ethan's laughing into his napkin. Matt looks like a dog that's been spooked by a loud noise and doesn't know which way to run.

"I'm Gwen. This is Raveena." Nose Stud, aka Raveena, finally arrives at the table. Gwen hip-bumps Raveena. "Told ya he's been on TV."

Raveena is not impressed. She stands with her arms folded in front of her. She clearly would rather be anywhere else. But I'm having fun.

"Where are my manners?" I say. "Ladies, take a seat. Matt, scoot over so they can sit down."

Matt gives me a pissed-off look, but he scoots over. They squeeze in next to him.

"That's Matt, and this is Ethan." Everyone nods hello. Except Raveena. She's showing her protest by staring down the salt-shaker. I'm beginning to seriously crush on her.

"What are you guys doing in Hollyweird?" I ask.

"We're here for the game tomorrow," Gwen says.

It's then that I realize that they're both wearing Michigan sweatshirts. They must be here for the Rose Bowl.

"Go, Wolverines!" I shout.

"Go, Blue!" Gwen cheers. "You like Michigan?"

"Yeah, well, we go to 'SC," I say. "Since we're not in the game this year, we sure as hell don't want Washington to win."

"Trojans! Fight on!" Ethan raises his Coke. I clink his glass with my milkshake. I look over at Matt.

He's following Raveena's lead and staring down the pepper shaker. Finally, he takes a deep breath and clinks our glasses with his water. "Fight on."

"Matt's in film school. Ethan's pre-dental."

"I'm the sensible one," Ethan says. "Those two are the dreamers."

"I'm business," Gwen says. "But social entrepreneurship

business. Not Evil Corp business. Raveena is poli sci. She's a dreamer, too."

Raveena looks ready to have the floor swallow her whole. I have pity on her and change the topic. "How long are you in town?"

"Oh, a couple more days. We're going to Disneyland after the game. Aren't we, Vee?"

"We should really be heading back, Gwen," Raveena says. "It's getting late."

"We're here with a group from our dorm." Gwen helps herself to a couple of my fries. "We're kinda having a party at our hotel. Want to come?"

MATT

"This is a bad idea."

No one is listening to me. Ethan's in the back seat of the Beast, trying to clean up the pigsty that it's become in two days. The little green tree hanging on the rearview mirror isn't strong enough to cover up the stench of three guys in an enclosed space for too long, so Oscar spritzes his cinnamon breath spray in the front seat.

Gwen and Raveena stand at the corner, having a prolonged discussion. At least Raveena is on my side because I clearly hear her say, "I'm not getting in a car with three strangers!"

Raveena seems to have overlooked the fact that she and Gwen are strangers to us and I don't want them in my car. Most likely for very different reasons than Raveena has in mind, but the fact remains it's a bad idea.

But Oscar and Ethan are gung-ho for going to this party, which isn't at a nearby hotel, as I originally thought, but in Pasadena. I don't know how far away Pasadena is, but it seems far from the way Gwen said it.

I hear Gwen repeating her argument about how much money

they'll save if they ride with us instead taking an Uber, especially now that it's surge pricing. She also reminds Raveena that Uber's entire business model is to have people get in a stranger's car. Raveena sighs loudly as she pushes a strand of hair behind her ear. I believe she is starting to crack under the peer pressure.

"Don't we have to check into our hotel?" I ask Ethan. "Won't we lose the room?"

"Oh, we've probably lost it by now," he says.

"What?"

"Dude, chillax," Oscar says. "Gwen said we could crash with them."

Now it's my turn to sigh loudly.

"I'm driving," I say.

"Cool." Oscar tosses me the keys. Gwen and Raveena walk over to the Beast. "Who wants to ride shotgun?" he asks them.

Raveena nudges Gwen.

"Um, we'll both sit in the back, if that's okay," Gwen says.

"No problemo." Oscar opens the passenger door for them, and they climb into the back. Oscar follows them in. Even though Gwen is taller, she's the one who ends up sitting in the middle, her knees almost to her chin as she settles in over the hump.

"What am I supposed to do with this? I don't want to litter," Ethan whispers to me. He holds an armload of trash in fast food take-out bags. I glance around. There are no trash cans nearby.

I take another deep breath. I don't want to litter either, but it's the least of my worries. "Leave it in the alley. It'll be fine."

Ethan tosses the bags toward the alley. They scatter as they land a couple of feet short, but Ethan is already heading for the passenger seat.

I get in the car and adjust the seat and mirrors. "Everyone's seat belt is on?" I ask.

"Yes, Dad," Oscar says. Gwen stifles a laugh. I can see in the rearview mirror that Raveena rolls her eyes.

As I pull away from the curb, Ethan puts in a cassette tape. "The Promise" begins to play.

OSCAR

"Jesus Christ!" I shout.

Someone throws a pillow at me. Maybe it was the white guy with bad acne. Parker, I think? I've said "Jesus Christ" as my answer every round. I figure that eventually I'll be right.

The others on our team shout out names like Eve and Queen of Sheba.

"Time's up!" Matt says.

"It was Absalom!" Gwen points the stylus at the stick figure on the iPad. The drawing looks like a woman floating in a tree. "See the long flowing hair? Caught in the tree?"

"Then you should have drawn the three darts in his heart," Parker says. "I thought it was Eve and the Tree of Life."

"Then the tree would have had apples!" Gwen says, her hands on her hips. Damn, that girl doesn't like to lose. But everyone laughs, including Gwen. And there's Matty, his head back, howling with laughter. I don't think I've ever seen him laugh before.

"We won! We won!" a short white girl chants as she jumps up and down. She gives Matt and the other people on her team a high five.

"I demand a rematch!" Gwen says.

"Okay, but let's take a break first," the Asian guy with big ears says. Owen? There are about eight people in the Michigan crew, and I only remember the names of a couple of them.

Raveena, who was on my team, nudges my shoulder. "Can we talk? In private?" she whispers.

I give her my best shit-eating grin. I lean in and whisper back, "Did I hear you right? You want to talk privately? To me?"

The look she gives me would freeze the sun. She doesn't say anything but walks out of the hotel room as though she expects me to follow her.

Of course I do.

ETHAN

Levi:
How's the party?

Me:
yawn

Levi:
???

Me:
I'm at a Comfort Inn in Pasadena
with a bunch of Christians!

Levi:
!?!

Me:
I thought going to a party with college
students would mean 🍺.
I thought it'd be a crazy night.
They're playing Bible Pictionary.

Levi:
I am dead.

Me:

Matt's team won.

Levi:

Can't. Stop. Laughing.

Me:

I told them I'm Jewish, and they promised
to do only Old Testament clues.

Levi:

That's fair.

Me:

I passed.

Levi:

I won't tell you how awesome
this Google party is.

Me:

I hate you so much.

Levi:

Me:

They're super nice, though. Almost
as nice as Mormons.

Levi:

There's a bouncy house and
a snow cone machine.

Me:

eye roll

Levi:

Two words: chocolate fountain.

Me:

They have Fritos and a case of
Mexican Coke. They call it pop.

Levi:

There are pony rides outside.

Me:

👖🔥

Levi:

LOL. You're right.

There's no chocolate fountain.

Me:

I thought something smelled funny. 😄

Levi:

Nice callback!

Me:

Oscar's gone off with a girl.

Levi:

Don't you mean Manuel?

Me:

PUHLEEZ! He didn't even give me a chance
to come up with my own fake name.

Levi:

You'd make a good Seth.

Me:

I was going to say Seth!

Levi:

I know you so well. 😉

Me:

😍

Levi:

Hey, we're almost at midnight.

Me:

10

Levi:

9

Me:

8

Levi:

7

Me:

6

Levi:

♡♡♡♡♡

Me:

👍👍👍👍

Levi:

😀😀😀

Me:

👽👽

Levi:

🤖

Me:

Happy New Year! 🤩

Levi:

Happy New Year! 🐱

MATT

I wish I could tell Mom about tonight. She'd like Gwen and the others. They're not like the kids in youth group who only want to play videogames and text each other even when they're sitting across from each other. Maybe because they're college-aged and more mature. Duncan has said that college is where I belong, where I will finally find my crew. I never thought my crew might be in Michigan.

But I can't tell Mom because I'm not supposed to be in Los Angeles and because my presence here is predicated on a lie. When I called her earlier, I told her that we were at a hotel in Moab, Utah, eating pizza and watching a *Twilight Zone* marathon on TV. The need to confess the truth is becoming overwhelming.

I've also lied to these people who have welcomed us into their group. I want to tell them the truth, too, but I don't want them to think badly of me. Especially Gwen. She's so friendly and comfortable around people that it makes me feel at ease around her. Not like the girls at youth group, who are all nice girls, but I never know what to say to them.

So I let the lie fester and tell myself that it's not fair to expose Ethan and Oscar without their permission.

Our team has beaten the others by a large margin, and a rematch has been demanded. But we're taking a break for the countdown. There's nine of us in the hotel room, most of us clustered on the two double beds to watch the ball drop in Times Square. Ethan sits on the floor against the closet door, texting. I don't know where Oscar is. Or Raveena.

"Want a pop?" Gwen asks as she sits next to me.

I deduce that by *pop* she means one of the Mexican Cokes she holds in her hand. I nod, even though I don't like them. They're too sweet.

"Not exactly the New Year's you were planning, right?" Gwen says.

"Even better," I say.

Gwen laughs. I like the way she laughs. It's throaty, almost a rumble. "I wasn't going to approach you guys at the restaurant because Vee was so dead set against it. But maybe God wanted us to meet, ya know?"

I smile at the thought. "Mysterious ways and whatnot."

Gwen laughs again. "Exactly!"

I realize that our thighs are touching. I know that on the other side of me sits Parker, an engineering major with acute acne, and his thigh is touching my other thigh. Yet that lacks the same feelings of excitement and anxiety as having Gwen's thigh next to mine.

I normally would have described the type of girl I was attracted to as Natalie Portman in the *Star Wars* prequels: petite, elegant, and protective of her loved ones. Gwen is tall and lanky and fiercely competitive, at least when it comes to Bible Pictionary. Sitting this close to her, I notice that her lower teeth are slightly crooked, and she has a constellation of faint freckles across her nose that disappear under the frames of her tortoiseshell eyeglasses.

"The rest of the group wanted to go to see the Rose Parade floats line up, but I'm like, heck no, let's go to Hollywood. I mean, our group went there yesterday, but the tour bus only stopped for, like, five minutes. But Vee, she said she'd go with me, and it kinda worked out nice." Gwen pats my knee for emphasis. It's the briefest of moments, but it feels electric.

"Where is Raveena?" Parker asks.

"I think she went to get some fresh air," a girl says. She gave everyone on our team high fives after we won, and I'm pretty sure her name is Sarah.

"She's going to miss the countdown," Parker says.

"Her loss," Gwen says, giving me a nudge in the ribs. "I think he was hoping to kiss Vee at midnight," she whispers as she leans in to me. Her breath smells like Fritos, yet not in a bad way.

"Ten!" the group shouts.

"Nine!" I join them.

"Eight!" I wonder if Gwen said what she said about Parker because she wants me to kiss her.

"Seven!" I wonder if I need to ask for consent for a New Year's Eve kiss.

"Six!" I imagine our lips touching.

"Five!" I imagine other things touching and immediately feel remorse about it.

"Four!" I wonder if I'm misreading the situation.

"Three!" I think about what Oscar would tell me to do in this situation.

"Two!" I think about what Ethan would tell me to do in this situation.

"One!" I take a deep breath.

"Happy New Year!"

Everyone clinks their Mexican Coke bottles together. Then they start giving hugs and some are even kissing.

Gwen gives me an awkward side hug. Before she can pull away, I say, "Can I?" and she gives a slight nod of her head. I've seen the perfect kiss so many times in movies that I know enough of the mechanics to tilt my head so I don't hit my nose with hers. I close my eyes and pucker my lips.

I kiss her.

She obviously isn't expecting it. Her lips aren't puckered and I can feel her teeth. A hot rush of humiliation overwhelms me. Of course she wasn't expecting it. I only said, "Can I?" as though she would know what I meant by that. What I thought was a nod was probably just her waiting for me to finish a coherent sentence.

I break away and take a swing of the Mexican Coke. "Here's to the new year," I say after I swallow, as though the kiss wasn't my very first kiss, as though it wasn't an abject failure.

OSCAR

"So what's up?" I ask.

Raveena and I arrive at the pool, all lit up and bright blue. We scout out a couple of plastic lounge chairs next to each other. It's gotten colder and I'm freezing. I put my hood up and dig my hands into my pockets. Michigan girls must define cold differently because Raveena takes off her sweatshirt and wraps it around her waist. She wears a Michigan T-shirt underneath it.

"Why?" she asks me.

"Gonna need you to narrow that down for me." She's been ignoring me the entire night. Even during Bible Pictionary, even though we were on the same team.

"Why did you lie to Gwen?"

"What lie?"

"There's more than one?"

"Possibly. I wasn't really keeping track."

"I know who you are." She says it with the finality of a jury verdict.

"I would love for you to let me in on that particular secret."

"Are you making a joke?"

"Not entirely." I lean back on the lounge chair and put my hands behind my head as I stretch out. My body language could not be more obvious that I don't give a shit.

"You're Oscar Vargas, not Manuel whatever. My mom interviewed your mom for *Eye on Ann Arbor* during her last book tour."

"Cool, cool."

"You don't seem surprised that I know."

"Dude, I've been waiting for someone to try to google me and call me out. I didn't think you'd be discreet about it, though. You should've said something back at the diner."

"I wasn't completely sure then."

"You gonna tell the others?" I don't care if I look like an asshole, but I don't want Ethan and Matt to take any heat. Especially Matt.

Raveena pushes a strand of hair behind her left ear. She probably doesn't realize it, but it's a tell. She's been doing it all night, whenever she's making a decision.

"No. But I still want to know why you lied."

"I thought that was obvious. Would you want to be me?"

"You lost your dad. So did I."

That hits me in the gut. But if I can't deal with my own shit, how can I deal with another person's pain? By doing what I always do. Push them away. "Oh, was your dad killed by a school shooter, too?"

"No, it was a car accident last winter. There was a patch of ice and he hit a pole." She says it simply, not taking the bait that my trauma is bigger than hers. This is not a contest about who is more broken. She's not like the McDonald's cop or the other people who just want to share their own personal grief without actually giving a shit about me. This is . . . different.

The fact that she didn't narc on me tells me that she doesn't deserve my bullshit. I sit up to face her. To tell her the truth. "So you remember how it was afterward, when people would see you and it'd get quiet because they didn't know what to say. Finally they would say, 'Sorry,' and you'd say, 'Thanks.' Then it was over for them. But you have to live with the loss every single moment."

"Yes, but it meant something that they recognized the loss."

I ignore that because I haven't gotten to my point yet. "Now imagine that instead of only your friends and neighbors telling you, 'Sorry,' it's everyone on the Internet. And their thoughts and prayers do nothing to stop the nightmares."

She sighs. "The sorrys did make me feel numb after a while."

sorry won't bring your dad back.

Raveena reminds me of Kayla. She sees beyond my assholery, and she's still sticking around. For a moment I think I can show her the letter and she'll understand. But I hardly know her. It's too much to ask of a stranger. So I don't.

"My grandmother just died," I say. "I'm sad she's gone and I'm sorry I didn't get a chance to say goodbye. That's grief. But what happened to my dad—and your dad—that kind of sudden, violent death causes trauma. And most people don't get that. They think I should pull myself together, I've had enough time to get over it. Like trauma works that way."

"You lied because you want to keep people at arm's length,"

she says, tucking her hair behind her left ear. "You don't want them to know who you really are. And I don't mean your name and your backstory. You're scared of people judging you."

"I thought Gwen said you were poli sci, not psych."

"We're all scared of something." Raveena sits on the lounge chair, her legs tucked underneath her, her arms hugging her torso, like she's trying to disappear into herself.

"What are you scared of?" I ask.

"I'm afraid of my mom being alone, now that I'm at college. I'm afraid of forgetting my dad. Little things, like what he smelled like." She closes her eyes for a moment, as though she's trying to capture the memory.

"What did he smell like?"

"Old books and peppermint. He was an archivist at the university. He liked those red-and-white striped peppermint candies. He kept them at his desk."

"I don't remember what my dad smelled like. But I think of him whenever I smell creosote bushes. They smell like rain, like monsoon season, all musky and earthy. My dad loved monsoon season."

"Hold on to that. And all the other memories you can."

"There's one . . . I've never told anyone this before." There's a stinging in the back of my eyes and a tightness in my throat. Raveena waits until I'm ready to go on. "My dad's driving me to school and quizzing me on state capitals because I had a test that day. He made it like a game show, telling me about the fabulous prizes I'll win, like a lifetime supply of knowledge and a brand-new confidence. It was kind of dorky, but that was my dad. I get out of the car at the drop-off, and he says he knows I'll do great. Those were the last words he said to me."

"That's a good memory. It's sweet. The last thing my dad said to me was, 'How can a haircut cost so much money? My barber can cut your hair for twenty dollars.' I've been writing everything down in a journal." She pushes her hair behind her left ear again. "My mom and I are going to a grief counselor. I've heard before some of the stuff you said about the difference between grief and trauma. And I had no idea that there are these different grief theories. Five stages of grief, four tasks of mourning, you got to do your grief work, it's a process, it's a journey. I find it overwhelming."

"My mom ran with that. Posted all the inspirational quotes on Facebook. Read all the books. Then she started writing her own books. Keeping busy became her way to avoid dealing with the grief. But I'm the one she makes go to a therapist."

"Your mom is trying to make a difference because of what happened. What about you?"

I shrug. "I just try to get through the day."

Raveena hugs herself tight. "Another thing I'm afraid of is not living a life my dad would be proud of."

She's hit me in the gut again. But harder. I look down at my hands because I'm too much of a fuckup to face Raveena. Dad's last words to me were actually "Don't worry, you'll do great." But I am not doing great, Dad.

The only sound is the pool filter pumping away

"Who are those other two guys?" Raveena finally asks.

I am fucking relieved to talk about anything else. "Ethan and Matt. Real names. They're my cousins. We're on our way to New Mexico."

"Are they actually at USC?"

"Nope. We're all high school seniors. Ethan's not even eighteen yet."

"Are you kidding me?" Raveena's complete surprise makes me laugh.

"It's not like you were serving alcohol to minors. Though we were kinda expecting that when Gwen invited us to this rager."

Raveena smiles. It's almost as glorious as one of Kayla's smiles. "We should probably go back in. It's almost midnight."

But she's wrong. It is midnight. There are shouts and noise-makers from the hotel rooms. Somewhere nearby, people are setting off fireworks.

We watch them in silence.

JANUARY 1

ETHAN

I want waffles.

I can't sleep and I want waffles.

Matt and I are sharing a bed again. Parker and Owen are asleep in the other double bed. They were nice to let us crash with them, but Parker has a sinus thing that kept me up most of the night.

I put on my glasses. It's still dark outside, but I'm used to getting up early to practice the violin. I'm going to have to do a marathon practice when I get home to make up for the days I've missed.

I carefully get out of bed so I don't wake up Matt, then grab my coat and shoes to go look for Oscar. I haven't seen him since last year. Ha, I crack myself up.

The hotel is horror-movie quiet as I walk through the lobby. I see the sign for the gym and hear a continuous loop of a mechanical squeak and a hard thudding noise. Someone must take their physical fitness super seriously if they're exercising this early on New Year's Day. I peek through the window in the door. Raveena is on the treadmill.

I go inside and stand in front of her machine. "Happy New Year."

"What?" She takes out her earbuds, but keeps running. She's listening to Brahms's Hungarian Dance No. 5 in G Minor. I give her points for her musical taste.

"Happy New Year," I repeat.

"Happy New Year."

"Do you know where Oscar is? He's not answering his phone."

She manages to shrug and run at the same time. "Last I saw him was at the pool."

I walk around for ten minutes before I discover that the pool is on the roof. I find him asleep on a lounge chair. I shake his shoulder until he wakes up.

"What time is it?" he says, yawning.

"A little past six."

He looks up at the moon that's still hanging low in the slate gray sky. "In the morning?"

"I want waffles."

Oscar looks over at the empty lounge chair next to him. He shakes his head. "Yeah, you know, I could go for waffles, too."

"Should we wake Matt?"

"Nah, let him sleep." Oscar stands up. Something drops to the ground when he does. He picks up a Michigan sweatshirt. It's not rocket science to figure out that Raveena put it over him while he was sleeping.

"What happened with you and Raveena?"

"She knows I'm full of shit."

"So I can stop calling you Manuel?"

"No, Manuel still lives. Raveena's cool. She's not going to tell the others."

"Damn."

"You said something about waffles?"

"We could Uber to a Denny's."

Oscar takes out his phone. "Done."

OSCAR

"Matt is going to kill us," Ethan says with his mouth full of waffles.

"He's fine. He's probably still asleep."

"I know, but . . ." Ethan points his fork at me for emphasis, then shrugs.

"What?" I ask. The waitress refilling my coffee cup could not give a shit about our conversation. But Ethan waits until she walks away.

"I thought we were all in this together. Like the Three Amigos or something. I feel bad ditching him."

"We're not ditching him. We're having breakfast."

"Yeah, like, thirty miles away from where he is."

"You're the one who wanted to go to the beach."

"I know, but still . . . we should be looking out for each other. My mom said we need to keep the family together now that Grandma Lupe is gone."

"Dude, our family has never really been together."

"I'm pretty sure that was my mom's point. If we don't start being a family now, then when? We should have at least given Matt a choice."

Here I was, thinking I was doing a nice thing for Ethan by having the Uber driver take us to Denny's in Santa Monica, only a ten minute walk to the beach. But now I'm an asshole. Again.

"Okay, you have a point," I say. "So it's up to you whether to tell him we came here."

"He's going to ask where we went."

"All you have to say is, 'We went to breakfast.' End of conversation."

"You're a master of lies of omission," Ethan says before chowing down on another mouthful of waffles.

"It comes in handy."

There's a long pause while we eat. I think about what Ethan said about family. A couple of days ago, no matter how we were related, Matt and Ethan were nothing but names to me. I'm not sure what exactly we are now, but I don't think it's strangers anymore.

"You still wanna go to the beach?" I ask.

"Might as well. It's right down the street."

I raise my coffee mug in salute. "Lies of omission it is."

MATT

I floss my teeth. I try to organize my thoughts as I do, but they remain chaotic. The kiss with Gwen. Lying to my parents. Where Oscar and Ethan could have gone.

I'm annoyed that they didn't wake me up, but it was good to sleep a few hours without Ethan kicking me. If only Parker didn't have sinusitis, I could have gotten a deep sleep.

There's a knock on the bathroom door. "You almost done?"

I open the door. Owen wears only his boxer shorts. "About time," he says as he slips past me and closes the door. A few seconds later, I hear the shower running.

"Thanks again for letting us stay with you guys," I say to Parker. He's putting his sneakers on while sitting on one of the beds.

"It's no big deal," he says. "Gwen's always picking up strays."

"What does that mean?" I don't think it's good.

He shakes his head. "Nothing."

"It must, or you wouldn't have said it."

He takes a minute to tie his laces before he looks up at me. "Gwen, she's friends with everyone. She's a lifeline for the socially awkward and nerdy. None of us would have come on this trip if it hadn't been for her. She can be pushy, but she has a big heart."

"So me and my . . . my friends, we're just her latest strays?"

"Don't get me wrong, she's not the kind of person who drops friends when she makes new ones. But don't read more into it than it is."

Parker saw the kiss. He's letting me know that I'm nothing special.

I nod. It's for the best. I can't get involved with Gwen when I've done nothing but lie to her.

ETHAN

"Oh crap, the water's cold." I step back quickly before the waves crash over me. I'm still wearing what I normally sleep in, sweatpants and an old camp T-shirt. I've rolled up the sweatpants, and white, foamy water licks my bare feet as they sink into the wet sand.

The sun is finally out and it's beautiful. There are palm trees and joggers and people walking their dogs. There's also a homeless guy digging through a trash can. That's pretty much a microcosm of the world.

I take a selfie while I'm ankle deep in the Pacific Ocean. I send it to Jiwon and Levi, although I don't think they'll be awake for a couple more hours.

I trudge through the sand, which is also cold, to the spot farther up the beach where Oscar's sitting with my shoes and coat. "Don't you want to go in?"

Oscar shakes his head. "I'd rather watch the waves."

"That's my favorite thing about the beach, too." I join him in following the crest and fall of the waves. It's almost like a lullaby.

A thought comes to me. "Don't you think it's weird that our moms left Portland to live in the desert?"

"After spending a few days in Portland, it makes complete sense," says Oscar.

"Yeah, but why not the beach? Or the mountains or Kansas?"

"No clue. Unless it's because people who don't like what they have want the opposite. Sometimes people are just contrary as fuck."

I nudge his shoulder with mine. "You think?"

He nudges me back. "Asshole," he says, but he's smiling. "We should head back. Matt must be up by now."

I do my best to brush the sand off my feet and put on my sneakers. "Oscar?"

"Yeah?"

"Thanks for bringing me to the beach."

He shakes his head, but he's still smiling. "I'll get us an Uber."

My phone pings. Levi is awake.

Levi:
You're adorbs, frolicking in the ocean.

Me:

I'm adorbs, period.

Levi:
You're not the only one with the power of adorbs.

Levi sends me a photo. It's him at the Google party with his arm around a guy with a ginger starter beard and wearing a black beanie. Is that his friend Jake? It must be. Levi wouldn't do that with some rando. Is Levi saying they're both adorable?

Or just Jake? Was his arm around Jake only for the photo? Or was it something more? Why won't my brain stop thinking these thoughts?

Me:

How do you know Jake again?

Levi:

We go to the same temple. Known him forever.

How can I compete with someone he's known forever? "Dude, Uber's here," Oscar calls out.

Me:

G2G.

MATT

"What happened to your friends?" Gwen scoots over at the table so I can sit next to her, even though the entire Michigan crew is already squeezed together around it.

I put my plate of bacon and eggs down, careful not to bump Owen, who is busy putting cream cheese on his bagel. The breakfast room is at capacity with hotel guests loading up their plates and filling their coffee cups. I had to wait five minutes for the staff to put out more bacon.

"Ethan texted me that they went to get waffles."

"Oh, shoot, they could have had breakfast here," Gwen says. "There's a waffle maker over there." She points to one side of the room where a long line has formed. I am sure it would take more than five minutes to get a waffle.

"They must not have known."

"We're tailgating with some other Wolverines at the Rose Bowl," Gwen says. "You can join us if you want."

Neither of us has spoken about the midnight kiss, and that is fine with me. I want to believe that since Gwen is asking me to continue to be in her presence, maybe the kiss wasn't as horrible as I thought.

No, the kiss was truly horrible. But perhaps it wasn't entirely unwanted. Maybe she would even like an opportunity at a better one. But then I remember what Parker said. I'm only another stray.

Even if that wasn't true, I am still caught in a lie. She thinks I'm a USC student and that it's possible for me to spend the day with her.

"Sorry, we have other plans." These half-truths are making my stomach hurt. I can't even eat the bacon.

Oscar and Ethan walk in. Oscar is wearing his clothes from yesterday, and Ethan is still in his pajamas. Something weird is going on, and it makes my stomach hurt even more.

Gwen sees them, too, and waves them over. "Hey, guys, you could have had waffles here."

Oscar and Ethan look at each other. They are unsuccessfully trying not to laugh. There is no more room at the table, so they're hovering behind me. I don't know why, but I feel trapped.

"What else did we miss?" Oscar asks.

"I told Matt that you're welcome to tailgate with us," Gwen says. There is only one person at the table not enthusiastic in encouraging us to join them. Raveena has not looked up from her container of yogurt since Oscar arrived.

"Well, thanks, but we gotta get back to 'SC," Oscar says. "Unless, Matt, you wanna—"

"I already told Gwen we have other plans." I don't want to sound rude, but I could see the day slipping away if we agreed to go. I wouldn't get to see the campus and we'd never get to Santa Fe in time.

"Cool," Oscar says. "You gonna eat that bacon?" Without waiting for an answer, he takes a slice from my plate and pops the whole thing in his mouth. Then, while he's still chewing, he says, "We should head out when you're done."

At that, Raveena looks up. But only for an instant. Then it's back to her yogurt. Something happened between her and Oscar, that much is certain. But I have no idea what and I'm not sure I want to know.

"I'm ready," I say as I stand.

Gwen puts her hand over mine. Her fingers are warm and a little sticky from maple syrup. "Are you on ChatThat?"

"Um, no."

Ethan fake-coughs in his hand and whispers, "Phone number."

"But, uh, I can give you my phone number."

Gwen smiles as she hands me her phone. "Once you put it in my contacts, I'll text you so you'll have mine."

I enter the digits and hand the phone back to her. She types on it and almost instantly there's a ping in my back pocket.

I check the text.

Go Wolverines! 😊

I don't know if the emoji is for the Wolverines or for me. I am more confused than ever.

OSCAR

Matt is taking forever to say good-bye to the Michigan crew. He calls it "a church good-bye," which gets a big laugh from them.

Ethan's gone upstairs to change. I, unlike Ethan, did not have my mom do my laundry before we left, so I don't have any clean clothes to change into anyway.

I've been keeping an eye on Raveena, who went to throw out her empty yogurt cup. But it looks like she's using that as an excuse to bail. I follow her out into the lobby.

"Hey, Raveena!" I don't mean to shout like that, but she's almost to the elevators. It works, though. She stops and turns around.

"I almost forgot to give you this." I untie the Michigan sweatshirt from my waist and offer it to her. "Sorry about the sand."

There are half a dozen strangers in the lobby looking at us. I motion to a couple of empty chairs. Raveena pushes her hair behind her left ear. She gives an almost imperceptible nod. We sit down and our audience loses interest.

She takes the sweatshirt without saying anything. She stares at it bunched in her hands. She probably regrets telling me all that personal shit. It makes you vulnerable. I get it. I'll make it easy for her.

"Okay, then." I stand up. "It's been super awesome. See you around. Or not."

"Wait."

I wait.

"Sit down."

I sit down. I am starting to feel like a trained poodle.

"I've been thinking about our conversation last night," she says. "About being afraid of losing our memories of our fathers. The thing is, we're too willing to hold on to the pain. The pain is more real than our memories of them. And that's not right. I think . . ." She pushes her hair behind her left ear. "I think I can't hold onto the memories unless I give up the pain. I'm going to hold tight onto every scrap of memory because that's what my dad would want for me. Not the pain."

We're silent for a long time. Then I finally say it.

"My therapist says pain is the word we use for all the shitty stuff trauma makes us feel. The depression, the anxiety, the guilt, the anger, the fear—that's all pain. I don't fucking want to hold on to it, but I don't know how to let it go."

Raveena lets out a long breath. "I don't either. But I'm going to try. So, thank you for helping me figure that out."

Matt and the Michigan crew flood into the lobby and spot us. "Hey, you two, are we interrupting?" Gwen says, sitting on the arm of Raveena's chair.

Raveena stands and ties the sweatshirt around her waist. "Just discussing the secrets of the universe." She follows the others toward the elevator. "Good-bye, Manuel."

Gwen gets up and gives me a hug. It's unexpected, and I almost push her away. But she's surprisingly strong and holds me tight. "I'm glad I met you guys!" She finally lets go and runs to catch the elevator. "Have a blessed new year!"

My last sight as the elevator doors close is Raveena pushing her hair behind her left ear.

ETHAN

I thank Parker and Owen for putting up with us as I leave their hotel room and head for the elevators. My phone pings, and I still don't know what to say to Levi. He told me he was going to be with Jake at the Google party, but I didn't know Jake was going to be cute. Ugh, I don't want Levi know how insecure I am.

But it's not Levi.

Dad:
Hi!
It's Ruby.
Dad is helping me.

Me:
Hi, Ruby. 😉

Dad:
Happy New Year.

Me:
Did you stay up late?

Dad:

YES!

I got to see the ball drop.

> **Me:**
>
> Cool beans.

Dad:

When you come home?

> **Me:**
>
> Tomorrow.

Dad:

Yay!

Luv u.

> **Me:**
>
> Luv u, boogerface.

Dad:

Don't call your sister boogerface.

> **Me:**
>
> Dad?

Dad:

Yes.

> **Me:**
>
> Ruby loves it. It's our thing.

Dad:

Since when?

> **Me:**
>
> A couple of months.

Dad:

She says it's OK and you're a poopypants
(her words, not mine).

Me:

It's part of our thing.

Dad:

So why are you in California?

Me:

???

Dad:

I got an email that you didn't check in
to your hotel last night and we still
have to pay for the room.

Me:

We made a slight detour.

Dad:

California is not a slight detour.

Me:

Matt wanted to visit USC. Don't tell
Aunt Norma or Uncle Dennis.

Dad:

I'll decide what to tell them.

Me:

You asked me to help Matt if I could. He
needs bigger horizons. But his parents
want him to go to a Christian college.

Dad:

Why didn't you make it to the hotel?

Me:

We stayed with friends.

Dad:

What friends?

Me:

Dad, don't freak out.

Dad:

Now I'm worried.

Me:

We met some college students and they invited us to a party. It turned out to be the most boring New Year's Eve party in the history of New Year's Eve parties. I think that's punishment enough.

Dad:

Not even close, son.
We're going to have a long talk about this when you get home.

Me:

I expected that. But everything is fine.

Dad:

It better be. Love you, poopypants.

Me:

Love you too.
BTW only Ruby can call me that.

MATT

Being at USC during winter break is like that sequence in *28 Days Later* when the protagonist walks around an empty London. I could shout "Hello" over and over, but there's no one to answer me. Ethan said it creeps him out, but I don't feel that way. I feel like the campus is, in this moment, for me alone. It's not likely I'll get a chance to have it all to myself again.

I drag Oscar and Ethan across campus, admiring the traditional-looking redbrick buildings, the plazas, and the athletic field, until we finally reach the School of Cinematic Arts. The entire complex is like a Mediterranean villa with terra-cotta tiles and stucco walls. I would love to be on the other side of those walls one day, in the company of people as eager to learn as I am. I know I may not get that chance, but at least I took the chance to be here now.

So far, Oscar and Ethan haven't complained. Ethan even took a group selfie of us at the Tommy Trojan statue. But the morning is almost over, and it's time to head out. We're wandering back to the parking lot when I suggest we take a break. The sun shines brightly, and it's almost too warm in my flannel shirt.

We stop in Queens Courtyard, where brick walkways radiate from the inverted fountain in the center. Oscar stretches out along the concrete edge of the fountain. Ethan takes a photo of him before he sits down next to him. I am too excited to sit.

"So, is it everything you hoped for?" Oscar asks me.

"I feel inspired." Even empty of students, there's an energy here that fills me with possibilities.

"It's a pretty campus and everything," Ethan says, "but it's in a shitty neighborhood."

Oscar sits up to punch him on the arm. "Don't throw shade because it's not as filled with hipster assholes as Berkeley is."

Ethan rubs his arm. "First of all, ow. Second of all, I'm merely making an observation of fact. No offense, Matt."

"None taken."

"What are you going to do if you don't get in?" Ethan asks.

Oscar punches him on the arm again.

"Stop with the hitting!" Ethan says. "What are you, twelve?"

"Don't ask him that, *pendejo*," Oscar says. "Not cool."

"I thought you didn't speak Spanish," Ethan says.

"Only the curse words."

"Of course."

"How about you ask him what he'll do when he gets in?" Oscar says.

"So?" Ethan says to me.

"Even though I wouldn't be a film major, I can still take production and screenwriting classes. I want to learn to create my own narratives. I've already written a couple of screenplays."

"What are they about?" Ethan asks.

"One's about a group of teens at the end of the world. I know it sounds like a thousand other movies, but mine is *Deep Impact* meets *The Breakfast Club*. There's also a little *THX 1138* in the underground scenes and a lot more cast diversity. That's *Eden's Echo*. The other one is about a kid whose dad works for the government and they move to Area 51. There's a bit of a hat tip to *E.T.*, but it's more in the vein of *Inception* and deciphering layers of reality. That's *Omega Point*."

"You're a sci-fi geek!" Ethan says. "I would one hundred percent watch your movies!"

"Is the falcon thing from one of those?" Oscar asks.

"What falcon thing?" Ethan says.

"I'm writing down some scenes with a falcon motif. I got the idea at Grandma's burial. Didn't you guys see a falcon swoop down and land on a statue?"

Ethan shakes his head, and Oscar says, "I saw a pigeon drop a load on my mom's rental car."

"Well, I saw the falcon. I don't know if the idea will go anywhere. I have to find out what a falcon represents first."

Ethan types something on his phone and then scrolls. "Let's see . . . oh, I like this one. A falcon is 'a symbol of vision and success.' Maybe Grandma was sending you a sign that you'd get accepted here."

"That's a nice thought, but I don't believe in signs like that. I believe in praying and trusting in God to give you an answer. So if I do get into 'SC, then I know for sure that filmmaking is the path I should take. But if I don't get in, I'm staying on the path my parents want."

"Well, that sucks," Ethan says. "I'm ninety-eight percent sure I won't get into Berkeley. But that doesn't mean I can't put a year or two in somewhere else and then transfer. Getting a defer-ment on the dream, not giving it up, right?"

"It's not that simple," I say. I've already betrayed my parents' trust by coming here in the first place. The weight of the respon-sibility to not disappoint them feels heavier than ever.

"Why not?" Ethan asks. "It doesn't have to be all or nothing. It could be now or later. You've got to be flexible to reach your goals. Plans can go sideways like that!" He snaps his fingers. "You felt some kind of connection when you saw that falcon. It's your symbol now, you can make it mean what you want." He leans back on the concrete edge of the fountain, a satisfied smile on his face, as though he's solved everything.

"It's not that simple," I repeat.

"If I were Oscar, I'd slug you on the arm," says Ethan. "But I will say this—it's as simple as you let it be, *pendejo*."

ETHAN

Levi:

Haven't heard from you in awhile.

Levi:

Can't talk? I thought you weren't driving today.

Levi:

Miss you.

I can't ignore his texts anymore. My phone was pinging every few minutes as we walked around USC. I still can't get over the photo of Levi and Jake. Jake can be physically close to Levi, and I can't. And that makes me jealous of Jake because he has the advantage of proximity. I know it's irrational, but here we are.

Matt feeds the Beast at the pump, and Oscar went to grab snacks at the mini-mart. This is our last stop before we leave LA, and it's the closest to alone I'll be for hours. I might as well do this now.

Me:

Miss you, too.

Levi:

Everything okay?

> **Me:**
>
> Why wouldn't it be?

Levi:

You seem a little off.

> **Me:**
>
> Just tired.

Levi:

What with all that Bible Pictionary.

He's trying to make me laugh, but I can't do the banter thing right now. I thought we could stay in our bubble of happiness, even if we were apart. But whatever fantasy I had of having a boyfriend has been crushed by the reality. I don't know when I'm going to see Levi again. I don't know what I'm supposed to do in a relationship. I don't know if I can handle this.

> **Me:**
>
> Can't compete with the bouncy house
> and the pony rides and Jake.
> TTYL.

MATT

"Hey, Mom." I tuck my phone between my shoulder and my ear as I pump gas. Oscar is picking up some drinks and snacks in the mini-mart, and Ethan is texting in the passenger seat of the Beast. We are almost ready to leave Los Angeles. I feel as though everything has changed, although I'm not sure what exactly has happened. All I know for sure is that I have to lie to Mom again.

"Happy New Year! You didn't stay up too late, did you?"

"Uh, not too late."

"At least it's an easy driving day today, right?"

"Right." According to Dad's schedule, we should be near the New Mexico border.

"Dad's flying into Albuquerque tonight. He should arrive around midnight. Is it too much to ask that you stick around the airport to pick him up? I'm not sure when your cousins' flights are, but maybe they can keep you company for a while?"

I take a deep breath. "Shouldn't be a problem." This is the biggest lie of them all. Los Angeles to Albuquerque is a twelve-hour drive without stopping. It's 12:11 p.m. now.

"Thanks, *mijo*. I'm staying another couple of days to clean out the house. But I have great news!"

"What?" I could use great news right now.

"Manuel's Taqueria is expanding! Carlos will manage the Portland restaurant, and we've decided to put the money from the sale of the house toward opening another one in Santa Fe! My sisters will be silent partners, of course, but I'll run it."

She sounds so happy. I don't how long it's been since I've heard her sound happy. "What does Dad think?"

"It'll be a lot of work, but this is something we used to talk about."

"You and Dad talked about opening a restaurant?" I am astonished to learn this.

"It was a long time ago, but he knows how much I always wanted a restaurant of my own."

Mom had a dream I never knew about, a dream she had to wait years for. But now it looks like she's finally getting it. Maybe she understands what my dream really is. Maybe that's why she encouraged me to apply to USC. "That's great, Mom."

"Love you, *mijo*. Traveling mercies."

I'm going to need every mercy possible if I'm going to get to Albuquerque in twelve hours flat.

OSCAR

Matt looks dazed as he stands at the pump. I wave my hand in front of his face. "Cuz, wake up."

He looks at me, but he doesn't see me. Something is wrong. I lightly put my hand on his arm. "Matty?"

He blinks and takes a deep breath. "I am so screwed."

That's cursing for Matt. Something is definitely wrong. "What's the matter?"

"I'm supposed to pick up my dad in Albuquerque. There's no way we can get there in time."

Ethan joins us by the pump. "Wait, what?"

"How long is the drive?" I ask, ignoring Ethan.

"Twelve hours. His plane arrives at midnight."

"With the time difference, don't we gain an hour?" Ethan asks.

"I forgot about the time difference!" Matt's misery has Ethan and me exchanging worried looks. Matt takes another deep breath. "We lose an hour because New Mexico is mountain time, not Pacific time."

"No, dude, we can do this." I hold up the bag of Slim Jims and

Red Bulls I bought. "We power through it. Completely doable, right, Ethan?"

Ethan is checking his phone. "Uh, maybe not. It looks like there's snow in Needles. The I-40 is closed there."

Matt hangs his head in defeat.

"Hold on," Ethan says, still looking at his phone. "We can take the I-10 to Phoenix and then a couple of highways take us to the I-40 in Holbrook. That route is only supposed to take twenty minutes longer than the way through Needles."

"Twenty minutes?" Matt asks, hopeful.

"Yeah, Matty," I say, "we'll haul ass and get you there in time."

"Will there be bathroom breaks?" Ethan asks. "I'm not peeing into a Coke bottle."

"We'll have to fill up every few hundred miles," Matt says. "The Beast doesn't have great gas mileage."

"So you're in?" I ask.

Matt and Ethan nod.

"Then let's do this!"

"Three amigos!" Ethan shouts.

"That's a terrible movie," Matt says.

"Just say three amigos," Ethan says. "On one, two . . ."

"Three amigos!" Matt and Ethan shout. I might have, too.

ETHAN

We are flying along the I-10. I didn't know Matt had it in him to break traffic laws, but we're pushing ninety. I didn't know the Beast could go that fast.

"I've found a flight to Vegas that leaves Albuquerque at five forty a.m.," I tell Oscar in the back seat. "There's a stop-over in Phoenix. I can book both of us."

"Sounds good," he says.

"Are you sure you don't want us to leave you in Phoenix?" Matt says. "It seems a waste to fly back when we're going right through there."

"Dude, I am not bailing on this road trip," Oscar says.

"Damn straight, you're not," I say. "You're the one who made this happen."

Oscar shrugs. "Nothing better to do."

I hear a ping, but there's nothing when I check my phone. Another ping sounds. It's coming from Matt's coat.

"Matt, you're getting texted."

He keeps his eyes on the road. "I'm driving."

"You are a role model to America's youth," Oscar says. "You can learn something from your cousin, Ethan."

"Shut up, Oscar," I say as Matt's phone pings for a third time. "Give me your phone." I put my hand out and wait until he reluctantly pulls it from his coat pocket and gives it to me.

"Is it my mom?" he asks.

"It's Gwen."

"No shit!" Oscar exclaims.

I read the texts. "'Missing epic tailgate party.' And there's a photo of Gwen and a bunch of people in Wolverine sweatshirts standing next to a grill in a parking lot. 'Maybe next year we'll play USC.' And there are emojis of the victory sign and a football. The last one says, 'Hope to see you soon,' exclamation point, and a smiley face emoji."

"Dude," Oscar says, "did you hook up with Gwen?"

Matt's cheeks are blazes of red. "I kissed her."

Oscar leans over and punches him on the arm. "Way to go, Matty!"

"It was terrible. I did it wrong."

"She doesn't seem to be complaining," says Oscar.

"You have to text her back," I say.

"Maybe later," Matt says, "when I'm back in Santa Fe."

"You can't wait that long!" I say. "I'll text for you now."

Matt looks at me in panic. "What will you say?"

"Don't send her a dick pic," Oscar says.

"Shut up, Oscar," I say, and then to Matt, "How do you feel about her?"

Matt turns even redder. "I don't know. I just met her. I don't really know her."

"Is she a person you'd like to know better? Did you like being around her?" I ask encouragingly.

Matt takes a deep breath. "Yes. She's vivacious and confident in her faith."

"Do you want to bone her?" Oscar says.

"Seriously, Oscar, you're the worst person to give relationship advice," I say.

"You think you're an expert because you've had a boyfriend for a day?" Oscar says.

He doesn't know how insecure I feel being Levi's boyfriend, and I swallow hard. But I'll be damned if I let Oscar gloat about it. "Hailee and Rachel told me what you did at my bar mitzvah," I say.

"What did you do?" Matt asks.

"So one girl asks me to dance—"

"Hailee," I add.

"Whatever. And then we go make out by the kitchen. Later this second girl—"

"Rachel," I add.

"Yeah, her, she asks me to dance and then we make out behind the DJ's stage. I didn't know back then how much girls talk to each other. One told the other about me and then they both blamed *me* for making out with the other one. This was before my therapist told me I shouldn't hook up with girls who think I'm a wounded bird they can fix. Because even if it's consensual, it's not emotionally healthy for either of us. In theory, I get what he's saying, but when a girl offers, it's kind of rude to say no."

"You've just proved my point, Oscar. You're an asshole," I say. "Gwen's going to want a relationship with someone decidedly not an asshole."

Oscar gives me the finger and settles down in the back seat. I don't know when this insult banter started between us, but there's no heat in it. I think it's how Oscar shows affection. I guess it's our thing.

"Okay," I say, turning toward Matt, "she's obviously interested in you. She's keeping it in the friend zone because she doesn't want to get rejected, but she's leaving you an opening."

"I don't know about that. Parker said that Gwen is always making new friends and not to read anything into it."

"I don't remember which one Parker was," Oscar says, "but he probably could tell that you've got no game and thought he was doing you a favor."

"Exactly," Matt says.

"But Ethan's right," Oscar says. "These texts are an invite. She's into you."

"How do you know that from three texts?" Matt asks.

"It's the same tactic I used with Levi," I say. "We started by geeking out over the same fandoms. I was careful to keep the flirting light and playful. He starting flirting back and that's when I started thinking there could be more." Explaining this to Matt makes me feel shitty about the way I ended my last text with Levi. "So before I text back, I need to know how far you want to pursue this."

"I can't. I said I went to USC. I lied. I need to end it now."

"Dude, chillax," Oscar says. "I told Raveena the truth. I'll ask her to tell Gwen that lying was my idea, which it was. She might be mad at you for a little bit, but she'll get over it."

"Did you . . . hook up . . . with Raveena?" Matt asks.

"Don't make *hook up* sound like it's a criminal offense or something," Oscar says. "But no, we didn't."

"You were gone all night," Matt says.

"We talked. That's it."

"And she'll explain everything to Gwen?"

"Raveena's cool like that."

"I don't know how far I want to take this with Gwen. I don't know how to talk to girls."

"I've got your back, Matt," I say. "We'll keep it light for now, then see where it goes." I start tapping on Matt's phone, which is a piece of crap, but I'm not going to say that to his face.

"What are you writing?" he asks.

"'Looks like fun. But USC will take it next year.' Then an emoji of a football and a rose."

"Rose?" Matt asks. "It's that too romantic?"

"For the Rose Bowl. But she can read it as flirty if she wants to."

"Okay, send it," Matt says.

Before I can, the sirens start behind us.

MATT

I look in the rearview mirror. A California Highway Patrol car is behind us. I look at the speedometer. How long have I been going ninety?

I pull over to the shoulder. This stretch of the I-10 just before the Arizona border is a two-lane eastbound highway with nothing but desert scrub and barren hills for as far as the eye can see. There's hardly been any traffic for the last fifty miles.

I check the rearview mirror again. I see the CHP officer get out of the car and walk toward us. I keep my hands on the wheel like Dad taught me.

"Please, please, don't say anything," I say to Oscar.

"Dude . . ." He sounds insulted.

"Do you have drugs on you?" Ethan turns around to look at Oscar.

"Not *on* me. It's packed in the trunk. I told you guys I'd stay sober. And we're still in California. Recreational pot is legal here."

"Not if you're under twenty-one, you—"

Ethan is interrupted by the arrival of the officer, who taps on the driver's window.

I slowly raise my left hand off the wheel and lower the window. "Hello, Officer," I say, like Dad taught me. I slowly put my left hand back on the wheel.

"License and registration," she says without preamble. The officer is a white woman with blonde hair so tightly bound in a ponytail it looks painful. With her weather-beaten skin, it's hard to tell how old she is. She is stocky and has short, stubby fingers. She keeps them neatly manicured, though, with pale pink polish.

"The registration is in the glove compartment. Ethan, please get the registration out."

Ethan scrambles to open the glove compartment, and I can feel the officer tense up. She shifts back on her heels and puts her right hand close to her hip where her gun is.

Ethan finds it quickly and hands it to me. I hand it to the officer. "My license is in my wallet in my back pocket. I'm going to get it for you." I slowly reach for my wallet and pull out the license. I hand it to the officer.

"You were going over ninety," she says.

"I'm sorry." Dad taught me never to argue. Arguing is a sure way to get a ticket. Be humble. Be friendly. But most importantly, be respectful. Chances are, you'll get off with a warning. I've seen Dad do this across the Midwest and into Canada when I rode with him on long hauls. He never got a ticket.

"Where you headed?" she asks, peering into the car. It's not as messy as it was, but it still looks like a Circle K dumpster in the back seat.

"New Mexico."

"Says here the car is registered to Guadalupe Cardenas in Portland, Oregon."

"She was my grandmother. She passed away last week. I inherited her car."

"Who are your passengers?"

"My cousins."

"I want your IDs."

Ethan and Oscar hand over their IDs without a word.

"Stay put," she says before she walks back to her car with everyone's ID and the registration.

"Oh shit," Ethan mutters. "I've never been pulled over by a cop before."

"You still haven't," Oscar says. "Matt's the one who got pulled over."

I take a deep breath. "We do as she says, and it will be fine."

"Hey, Oscar, use your cop mojo on this one," Ethan says.

"What are you talking about?" Oscar asks.

"That cop at McDonald's practically asked for your autograph," Ethan says. "Let this one know who you and your mom are—"

"That would be a hell no."

"Why not?" Ethan asks.

"It doesn't work that way." Oscar says it with a firmness that means don't push it.

"What's taking so long?" Ethan turns around to look out the back window. His fidgeting is starting to grate on my nerves.

"She's checking if the car's stolen. Or if we have police records or any outstanding warrants," Oscar says.

"Oh shit," Ethan mutters again. After a long pause, he asks Oscar, "Do you?"

"Do I what?"

"Have a police record or any outstanding warrants?"

I turn around to look at Oscar, too. I hadn't considered those possibilities.

"No outstanding warrants."

"That only answers one of the questions," I say.

"The charges were eventually dropped."

"Oh shit," Ethan says, this time loudly. "What did you do?"

"I grew pot in an unused janitor's closet when I was at St. Catherine's Academy during my junior year. I told them it was a STEM project, but I got expelled—"

The officer knocks on the driver's window again. I roll it down.

"Step out of the car, please. All of you."

OSCAR

Matt looks like he's ready to puke. Ethan looks like he's going to shit himself. But I'm weirdly calm. Like it's happening to someone else and I'm just a bystander.

"You two, sit over there." The officer points to me and Ethan and then to the gravel shoulder of the road a few feet away where she can see us from the Beast.

"On the ground?" Ethan asks, horrified and insulted at the same time.

I tug on Ethan's sweater. "Be cool," I say as I lead him to the spot and sit down. Ethan kicks away a squashed plastic water bottle before he sits next to me.

The late afternoon sun hides behind the hills, and there's a bite in the air. I want to put my hands in my hoodie pockets to warm them up. But I know enough to keep them where the officer can see them.

The officer has Matt pop open the trunk.

"Don't you need a warrant for that?" Ethan asks.

The officer ignores him, but Matt gives him a look that clearly says, *Shut the fuck up.*

"Probable cause," I whisper to Ethan. "That's all she needs. But she didn't even need that because Matt agreed to it."

"Why would he do that?" Ethan whispers back.

I shrug.

"She better not touch my violin," Ethan mutters.

Now we have the officer's attention. She gives us a look that clearly says, *Shut the fuck up or I will shoot your sorry asses.*

I wait for her to tell Matt to unload the trunk and unpack the bags and suitcases. That's when the real fun will start. I still have some of the dime bag I bought from the busboy at Manuel's Taqueria. I'm under the legal limit, except I might have accidentally-on-purpose packed it in Matt's bag in the rush to leave the hotel in Berkeley. I needed to put it somewhere I couldn't get at it easily. I don't even want to think how pissed he'll be at me.

A Honda Civic drives by. A little brown girl in the back seat looks at us with wide eyes. She looks scared. Of us? Of the officer? I want to wave to her to let her know it's okay, but the car already sped down the highway.

I breathe a sigh of relief when the officer tells Matt he can close the trunk after she gives it a quick glance. Now I know she's fucking with us. She's got nothing, but she wants us to know she can make our lives miserable if she wants to.

The officer has Matt open the glove compartment. I'm close enough to see some of the mixtapes fall out and onto the passenger's seat.

The officer picks one up. "Where'd you get these?"

"My mom," Ethan says. "She made them when she was in high school."

The officer looks at the one in her hand. She doesn't mean

for it to be seen, but the slight stretch of her lips is definitely a smile.

She hands the mixtape to Matt. She starts writing out a ticket. "You got to watch your speed out here. A coyote runs out on the highway when you're going ninety and you brake too hard, it could put you in a tailspin or even flip your car. Seen it before."

"Yes, ma'am," Matt says, but I'm thinking, *Just hit the damn coyote.*

She hands the ticket and our IDs to Matt. She walks back to her patrol car without another word.

We stand around like idiots as we watch her drive off.

"Well, what tape is it?" Ethan asks.

Matt looks at it. *"Simon Le Bon 4Ever."*

"Thank god for Simon Le Bon," I say.

"I think my mom gets the credit," Ethan says as he heads for the passenger seat.

Matt's still shell-shocked. I snap my fingers in his face. "Yo, Matty! Want me to drive for a while?"

He shakes his head. "I prefer to drive." Matt looks down at the ticket. "This is my first ticket."

"Congratulations."

"This wasn't supposed to happen."

"Cuz . . ." I want to say something to make him feel better. But I can only think of one thing. "This will not be the last thing in your life that wasn't supposed to happen."

He takes a deep breath. "We're not going to make it to Albuquerque in time, are we?"

This is not the time for bullshit. "Probably not."

He nods like he finally gets it. It breaks my heart.

ETHAN

I put in the *Simon Le Bon 4Ever* tape. The synthpop beat of "The Reflex" starts up. I turn around to tell Oscar in the backseat, "You mocked me for my Eighties music. Mocked me! Bow down to your New Wave overlords!"

"We got lucky that cop likes mom music," he says. "She could have been a headbanger and then we would've been screwed."

I laugh, but then I remember. . . . "Gwen! I still haven't sent her the text!"

"It's probably for the best," Matt says, turning pink.

"No, no, we're doing this." I take Matt's phone out of my pocket and hit send. But he's still too upset about the ticket to focus on the big moment.

"I did everything my dad taught me to do when you get pulled over," Matt says. "He always got a warning. And I don't understand why she didn't give me the ticket straightaway. There was no reason to search the car."

"Seriously, dude?" Oscar says. "Your dad's white. But we're three young guys, each one browner than the last. She'd be derelict in her duty if she didn't fuck us over."

"You're not that brown," Matt says.

"I'm not that white, either," Oscar says. "And that's the problem. If people don't know what I am, then I'm whatever scares them the most. Mexican gangbanger, Muslim terrorist, it's all the same to them."

"Since you're so concerned about being racially profiled, have you thought about not wearing the hoodie?" I ask.

He gives me the finger.

"No, I mean it. People used to think I was Mexican when I wore long T-shirts and basketball shorts, which is what everyone wears at my school. Then Jiwon got me on this preppy kick, and I don't get followed in stores anymore."

"I am not wearing J.Crew sweaters."

"All I'm saying is that people judge you by your appearance."

"No shit, Sherlock."

"If you want to provoke a reaction, you can't complain when people react as expected," I say.

"Would you say that to Jiwon if she wanted to wear a hot little miniskirt?" Oscar says. "That's rape culture."

"That's not what I'm saying!"

"That's exactly what you said."

"Double standards are a completely different conversation," I say.

"Nope," Oscar says, "you don't want to admit that you owned yourself."

Sometimes Oscar is impossible.

OSCAR

Ethan gets out of trying to argue with me when his phone pings.

"Is that Gwen?" Matt asks.

"No, it's for me." Ethan checks the text. "Oh no," he says in a small, quiet voice.

"What?" I ask. From the look on his face, it looks like a break-up text.

"Mr. Taco died."

"The cat?" Matt asks.

"He's not just *the cat*," Ethan says, angry. "He's Mr. Taco! Grandma Lupe had him forever."

Matt continues to drive in silence. Ethan is near tears.

"That sucks, Ethan," I say because someone has to say something. I get why Ethan's upset. It's almost like losing Grandma again, and Ethan was closer to her than either me or Matt.

Ethan swallows hard. "He liked to put his purple mouse on my head when I was sleeping. And once he sneezed in my face."

"How did he get the name Mr. Taco?" I ask.

"One of the busboys found him as a kitten under the dumpster at the restaurant. I don't know why it was Mr. Taco and not

Mr. Enchilada or whatever. But the name stuck, and Grandma and Grandpa took him home."

"Was someone going to take him after Grandma died?" Matt asks.

"Mrs. Kaminsky offered to if the family didn't want him. But I guess he missed Grandma Lupe too much." Ethan's voice hitches at the end.

I think of Ruby sneaking pizza to Mr. Taco under the table. "How's Ruby taking it?"

"My mom's not telling her until she gets home. Your mom found him," he says to Matt. "She thought he was asleep in his favorite chair, but he didn't come running when she opened his can of food. That's when she knew he wasn't just sleeping."

"What are they going to do with him? Bury him in the backyard?" I ask.

"The vet's taking care of it." Ethan sighs. "This day went from possibilities to shit way too fast."

I want to say that's how every day is for me, but this isn't about me. It's about Mr. Taco. Really, it's about Ethan, who has had it pretty easy his whole life. He's used to having his tragedies be small.

"Ethan," I say, "Mr. Taco was a good cat and a good companion to Grandma Lupe, and he dealt the most fierce silent but deadly farts I have ever come across, man or beast."

Ethan does a double take. "What?"

"Dude, maybe it was the pizza, but that cat should have had a toxic waste warning on him."

Ethan fails at trying not to laugh. "I thought that was you."

"Me too," says Matt.

"I don't want to speak ill of the dead, but it was Mr. Taco. I think we should honor his legacy." I let one rip.

"Ew, Oscar, gross," Ethan says, laughing so hard he can barely get the words out. And then he squeaks one out.

"This is my car, you know," Matt says, not laughing at all. He rolls his window down.

"Come on, Matty, for Mr. Taco," I say.

"No."

"If you don't, I'll have to do another one," I say. "And I'm warning you, I'm full of Slim Jims. It might actually be a twenty-one gun salute."

Matt shakes his head. "You guys . . ." He gives in to the inevitable. "For Mr. Taco."

A volcano erupts.

"Damn, Matt, how long have you been holding that one in?" I say, choking on laughter and the smell. Mostly the smell.

"You asked for it," Matt says, innocent as anything.

"I didn't!" Ethan says. He rolls down his window, but he's still laughing.

Let's keep those tragedies small for as long as we can.

MATT

"What's that noise?" Ethan asks.

I was hoping that the squealing noise coming from the engine was only my imagination. "It means I need to pull over."

I stop the Beast in the emergency lane. I leave the headlights on and put on the hazard lights before I pop the hood. Once the sun went over the hills, it got dark quickly. We're about fifty miles outside of Phoenix and there's nothing here except an arroyo with a couple of cottonwoods.

"Did your mom leave the flashlight in the glove compartment?" I ask Ethan.

He digs around the cassettes and finds a small Maglite. "Didn't you and Uncle Dennis check the engine before we left?"

"Yes, but Grandma hardly drove outside a five-mile radius. We've gone over twelve hundred miles in two days. Lots of things could have gone wrong."

A couple of cars whizz by as I inspect the engine. Ethan and Oscar make a show of peering under the hood with me.

I spot the problem. "The fan belt's cracked."

"Can we duct tape it or something?" Oscar asks.

I shake my head. "If I don't replace the fan belt, the whole engine could be damaged."

"If we stop, we won't get to Albuquerque in time," Oscar says.

I know that down to my bones. There are always consequences to your actions. This is my consequence for lying to my parents. The first of more consequences to come. Not only consequences. There will be a reckoning. All my transgressions will be tallied up and I will have to answer for them.

"Where are we going to get a fan belt this late on New Year's Day in the middle of the desert?" Ethan asks.

"We're going to have to stop in Phoenix," I say.

OSCAR

"I don't want to stop in Phoenix." I did not mean to say that. I don't want them to ask why. But the Grandma in my nightmares knows who is waiting for me in Phoenix like some boogeyman.

I've thought about this for a long time.

"I don't want to stop, either," Matt says. "But we don't have a choice. We tried, though, right?"

You deserve justice.

"We can go to your house afterward, Oscar," Ethan says. "No offense, but you might want to think about taking a shower and changing into clean clothes."

I will not defend myself in any way.

The letter could be a trap. He could be coming after me.

It's up to you to decide if this is something you want to do.

But my cousins don't ask why I don't want to stop in Phoenix, and I know I wouldn't show them the letter anyway.

I catch sight of a bug kamikazeing into one of the headlights. Stupid fucking bug. Had a chance to get away but flies toward its stupid fucking death.

"I guess we're going to Phoenix," I say.

PART IV
PHOENIX

MATT

"Sorry, we're closed." The mechanic waves me away as I pull up to the Walmart Auto Center.

"It's not seven yet," Oscar shouts from the back seat. It's 6:52 p.m.

The mechanic stands with his arms folded, an exasperated look on his face. He's a Black guy in his thirties, bald and burly. He wears his Walmart shirt with a pair of blue chinos. "Come back tomorrow."

I put the Beast in park and jog over to him. "We're on our way to Albuquerque. We have to be there before tomorrow. All I need is a fan belt. I can put it in myself. Can't you sell me one?"

The mechanic's face flashes a look of sympathy. "We don't have any fan belts. We don't do that kind of maintenance here. Only tires and batteries and oil changes."

"Do they sell fan belts inside the store? It's open twenty-four hours, right?" Ethan asks. He and Oscar have also gotten out of the Beast.

The mechanic shakes his head. "They don't sell fan belts."

"Where can we go for the part we need?" I hear my voice

break as I ask. I have to calm down and think of this as an equation that has a solution.

The mechanic uncrosses his arms and rubs the back of his neck with one hand. "Maybe . . . hey, Hector, come over here!"

A skinny Latino mechanic in the same Walmart uniform walks over from the garage. He can't be much older than me. He eyes us with curiosity. "Yeah?"

"You got a fan belt for a 1988 Ford Thunderbird?" The first mechanic turns to me for a moment. "V-8 engine, right?"

"Yes, yes." I'm not sure what's going on, but I say a silent prayer.

Hector bobs his head as he thinks. "Yeah, pretty sure I do."

"I'll take it!" I shout.

He looks at me as though I were asking him for the moon. "I don't have it here. It's at home."

OSCAR

"Where you live?" I ask.

"Mesa," the skinny dude says.

"What part?"

"Near Stapley and Southern."

Of fucking course that's walking distance from my house. "We can follow you and drop off the car for you to fix," I say. "Hundred bucks for the whole thing."

"A hundred?" I hear Matt say faintly in the background. I ignore him. But he whispers in my ear. "We only need to buy it. I can replace it."

"You got the tools for that?" I whisper.

Matt shakes his head slowly.

"It's part of expenses," I whisper. "Ethan and me will pitch in."

Matt gets this resolved look on his face. "Okay, let's do it."

"Deal?" I say, putting my fist out toward the skinny dude.

He comes over and gives me a bump. "Deal."

"How long will it take?" Matt asks.

"Maybe an hour. Let me finish closing up and then you can follow me," he says as he walks back into the garage.

Matt approaches the older mechanic who's still standing in front of the entrance. "Thank you so much. You don't know what this means to me."

The mechanic breaks out into a smile. "Karma, right?"

"You say karma, I say grace of God," Matt says. But he's not smiling. He's still got that resolved look.

The older mechanic doesn't know what to make of Matt, but he looks amused. "It's all good."

The skinny dude comes back outside. "I'm ready. Bye, Eddie." He waves to the other mechanic and then heads for a white pickup truck. "Follow me!"

"If we had his address, we could put it in Google Maps," Ethan says.

I hurry after the dude. "Hey!"

He stops and waits for me. We're far away enough from the rest of the group that they won't hear.

"Hector, right?" He nods. "Did you go to Dobson High?"

"Yeah," he says. "I thought you looked familiar."

"You know Kayla Acosta?" I don't know why I'm asking this. Yes, I do. I want to know she's okay. I want to know she doesn't hate me.

"Sure. Sweet girl."

"You know how she's doing?"

"I graduated a couple of years ago. Haven't really kept in touch. Last I heard, she was working at the Applebee's on Baseline."

"Cool, cool," I say, as though this means nothing to me. "Why don't you give me your address just in case?"

He has to repeat his address five times before I get it right because my hands are shaking as I try to type.

ETHAN

We pass strip malls and subdivisions on the way to Hector's. The desert scrub, the mountains in the distance, it's almost like being home. Except Las Vegas has the glow of neon lights to keep it from being so boring.

I haven't heard from Levi in ages. Usually I know everything that's going on with him, but I have no idea where he is or what he's doing or who he's doing it with. How did I ruin a relationship in one day?

When Jiwon and I had our only fight, she didn't talk to me for two months. I can't bear the thought of not talking to Levi for that long.

Me:
Hey.

Levi:
Hey.

Me:
We had car trouble. We're going to some
guy's house and he's going to fix it.

Levi:

Sounds like the beginning of a horror movie.
Whatever you do, don't go to the basement.

Me:

What are you up to?

Levi:

What we do every night,
try to take over the world.

Me:

Watching Pinky and the Brain?

Levi:

Bingo.

Me:

Anyone with you?

Levi:

Just my mom.

Me:

Okay.

Levi:

Did that photo of me and Jake freak you out?

Me:

Maybe.

Levi:

Jake's straight, btw.

Me:

Like you've never had a crush
on a straight guy before.
Need I remind you of Randolph Mantooth?

Levi:

LOL!

Me:

But Jake's someone you actually know.

Levi:

Wait? Are you being serious?

Where is this coming from?

I honestly don't know, but it won't let me go.

Me:

I'm only saying the obvious.

You're so adorbs together, right?

Levi:

Wow.

Jealousy is not a good look on you.

Me:

I'm not jealous.

Levi:

If this long distance relationship is going to work,

you're going to have to trust me. Like I trust you.

I wish I trusted myself as much as Levi does. I'm so insecure I can't even tell him how insecure I am. I didn't want to ruin everything that was so perfect between us, but somehow I managed to do it anyway.

MATT

Hector parks his truck in front of a white bungalow with bougainvillea growing on a trellis against the porch. He waves me over to park under the carport. There's a broken-down car on jack stands already there, but there's room for the Beast behind it.

The motion detection lights in the carport flick on as I park. I hand the keys over to Hector. Then I notice what the other car is. "It's a Ford Falcon!"

"I knew you were a Ford guy," Hector says. "It's a '61. Needs a lot of work, but we'll get a good price for it when we're done."

"You restore old cars?" Oscar asks.

"Me and my brothers. They went to the movies with my mom, but they'll be home soon to help."

"You've worked on a Thunderbird before?" I ask.

"Yeah, but it was a '57. *Muy chido*. Don't worry, your baby is safe with me. I'll shoot you a text when I'm done."

He goes straight to work, popping the hood. I linger for a moment as Oscar and Ethan head for the sidewalk. I look back at the Ford Falcon. I am aware that the Baader-Meinhof phenomenon is when you notice something new and then it starts popping up everywhere. It doesn't mean there's a pattern, it only means that your brain is experiencing a frequency bias. But still . . . Ethan did say the falcon is my symbol now. What do I want it to mean?

I finally trail after them, but before I get too far, my phone rings. I could let it go to voicemail, but there would be no point to that. I might as well get it over with.

"Hi, Mom."

"Hi, *mijo*. I'm calling because Dad—"

"Mom, I have something to tell you. We didn't take the route Dad planned for us. We went through California and I visited USC. I got a ticket for speeding and now we're in Phoenix to get a new fan belt." I didn't mean to tell her all that, but once I started, I couldn't stop.

"Oh, *mijo*," Mom says. "Why?"

That's a good question. *Why?*

"I thought . . . I thought I couldn't let an opportunity go by. It was wrong not to tell you, but I'm not sorry I did it. I met a great group of Christians from Michigan, I loved seeing 'SC, and I shared my testimony with my cousins. Except for the ticket and fan belt, it's been an outstanding trip."

"Oh, *mijo*," Mom says again. "You're going to have to explain yourself to your father."

"I know." I know he won't see past the disobedience and lying. I know he'll never agree to USC now.

"Pray with me," Mom says. "Dear Heavenly Father, please help Matthew as he continues his journey. Keep him and his cousins safe. Let him open his heart to humility and obedience. In Jesus's name I pray, amen."

"Amen." Mom's gentle rebuke stings, but The Reckoning is still to come. It deserves capital letters, like the title of a post-apocalyptic movie.

"I called to tell you that Dad's flight has been delayed in Denver. There's a big storm coming. So you don't have to pick him up at the airport."

I close my eyes. If I hadn't confessed, there could have been a chance I made it home without them knowing I disobeyed. But now that I've confessed, I'm glad I did. Even though The Reckoning still waits for me.

ETHAN

It's only a fifteen-minute walk to Oscar's home, a cookie-cutter 1970s ranch house in a quiet cul-de-sac. A silver Jeep Wrangler sits in the driveway. The house is the only one on the block that doesn't have any Christmas lights hung up or a dried-out Christmas tree on the curb.

Even though the night air is chilly, the house is hot and stuffy inside. Oscar flicks on the air conditioner before he turns on the lights. I vaguely remember coming here after Uncle Gilbert's funeral. There's a sunken living room with brown shag carpet. Popcorn ceiling. Brown wood paneling on the walls. *Emergency!* might be on the TV right now, it's so Seventies.

"Imma take a shower. Order a pizza or something. Menus are on the fridge. Fire up the Wii if you want." He nods toward the game console and television in the living room.

"Your tech sucks," I say.

He raises his middle finger above him as he disappears down a hallway. Good ole Oscar.

Matt wanders into the kitchen and I follow him. It's the only room that looks renovated, and even that was at least ten years ago. The bright yellow paint and stainless steel appliances make the rest of the house seem sad. Forgotten. Lonely.

Matt scans the menus. "Chinese, Italian, Indian, Mexican, Thai . . . What do you feel like?"

"I don't know. Whatever. What do you want?"

"Truthfully, I'm tired of fast food. Do you think Oscar would mind if I cooked?"

"You cook?"

"My mom insisted I learn a few basics. But I don't love cooking like she does. She has the cooking gene like Grandpa Manny had."

"Yeah, I think that gene skipped this generation. My specialty is peanut butter and jelly sandwiches. They're Ruby's favorite. The secret is to add mini-marshmallows. Is there even any food in the house?"

Matt checks the fridge while I look in the pantry.

"Nothing much in the fridge, but there are frozen vegetables in the freezer."

"There's a lot of canned stuff." I look in the vegetable bin. "And some onions and potatoes and . . ."

That's not right.

There's a *gun* in the vegetable bin.

I look again.

There's a gun in the vegetable bin.

It takes a moment for all the pieces to come together and I see the signs. The mood swings. The self-medicating. The depression. The fact that it was Oscar's idea for the road trip. He didn't want to come to Phoenix. He didn't want to be alone. Because he knows this is waiting for him. Oh fuck, does he hurt that deeply that he's actually considering—

"What?" Matt asks.

"Suicide," I whisper.

MATT

Ethan's afraid to touch the gun, like it's a snake that might bite him. So I take it out of the vegetable bin. It's a Glock 43. I look to see if it's loaded. It's not. I notice a box of ammunition under the onions.

". . . the fuck?" Oscar says.

I turn around. He wears jeans and a plain black T-shirt as he stands in his bare feet. His hair is still wet.

"We were going to make dinner," Ethan says.

"Were you going to kill it first?" Oscar asks.

"Firearms should be stored in a safe place, preferably locked," I say, pointing the gun down toward the floor. "An empty vegetable bin is at least out of the way."

"Put it back," Oscar says.

"Do you know how to use it properly?" I ask.

"How hard is it to point and shoot?"

"Why do you have a gun, Oscar?" Ethan asks.

He ignores Ethan and keeps his eyes on me. "Put it back."

I do not.

"Why do you have a gun?" Ethan asks again.

"How do you know it's mine? Maybe it's my mom's."

"Because that makes no sense! She hates guns! She's made a career hating guns!" Ethan sounds mad, but I know he's scared for Oscar. I am, too.

"Is it your mom's gun?" I ask.

Oscar shakes his head. Droplets of water fall on his shoulders. "I bought it at a gun show."

"But why?" Ethan insists.

Oscar pulls a folded piece of paper from his back pocket. "Here."

I have no right to expect you'll read this. You can give this letter to your lawyer and have me busted for trying to contact you and breaking the terms of my probation. But I don't think you will once you understand why I'm writing you.

I didn't mean to kill Mr. Vargas. He was always kind to me. I've written you letters before letting you know that, but I threw them away. I've said sorry so many times, but it's a small word, an overused and almost useless word. Sorry won't bring your dad back.

I'm not asking for forgiveness because I don't deserve it. I wanted to believe in God because he would forgive me, but I don't believe in God anymore.

I've thought about this for a long time. You deserve justice. I'll be at the address on the envelope on New Year's Day. I will be alone. I will not defend myself in any way. It's up to you to decide if this is something you want to do.

T. A. G.

ETHAN

"Tanner Aaron Gibbs?" Even though I know it's a stupid question, I can't stop myself from saying it.

Oscar nods. He takes the letter from me and sticks it in his back pocket.

"When did you get it?" I ask.

"The week before Grandma Lupe died."

"That's messed up," I say. So much more of Oscar's behavior starts to make sense.

"What were you thinking, Oscar?" Matt asks it quietly, like he's trying to calm a trapped animal.

"What the fuck was I thinking?" Oscar runs his hands through his wet hair and then wipes them on his jeans. "I thought maybe I should get a gun to protect my mom and me. I thought . . . I thought a lot of crazy shit."

"Why didn't you report the letter?" I ask.

"If I did, then the lawyers and police and probably the media would be all over it, and I didn't want to deal with that. I just wanted to stay high during Christmas break and not have to deal with this shit."

"How did Gibbs get out on probation?" Matt asks.

"There weren't any laws that let a fourteen-year-old be tried as an adult back then. His lawyers were able to get him probation when he turned twenty-one. That was last month."

"The letter sounds like he wants you to get your revenge," Matt says.

"I used to be afraid of him when I was little kid, but by the time I was fourteen, I knew he was fucked up and I hated his guts," Oscar says. "Believe me, I used to imagine all sorts of horrible ways he could die. But I'm not going over there to kick his ass or blow his brains out or anything like that. Why the fuck can't he just leave me alone?"

"What are you going to do?" I ask. Because I think Oscar is holding back what he was really planning on doing with the gun. Matt and I can't leave him on his own. What we're going to do once the trip is over, I have no clue. Where is Aunt Elena, anyway?

Oscar shrugs.

"Are you thinking about killing yourself?" I ask.

Matt looks at me like that's the one question I shouldn't have asked, but it's the one that matters most.

Oscar shrugs.

"Oscar . . ." I want to sound calm like Matt did, but my voice is cracking like I'm hitting puberty again. "Oscar, I am here for you. You matter to me."

Oscar puts his head down and his shoulders begin to shake. Then I realize he's crying.

I put my arms around him.

He doesn't push me away.

OSCAR

I don't know how I end up on the couch, sitting between Ethan and Matt. At least I'm not crying anymore.

This is not how I wanted it to go down. I thought I could show them the letter and be all cool about it, like, *Hey, look at what this asshole sent me*. I didn't expect I'd be so fucking emotional.

Ethan's saying something on his phone, not talking to me, and I'm not really paying attention. Until I hear him say, "Aunt Elena."

"You called my mother?" I'm standing up now, though I don't remember doing that.

"I called *my* mother," Ethan says, ending the call. "She's going to talk to your mom."

"Oh shit." I am sitting down again, but I don't remember doing that, either. I lay my head against the back of the couch and stare at the popcorn ceiling.

"I asked if you can come stay with us in Vegas for a while. She said okay."

"Did you tell her about . . ." The letter? The gun? I can't say either of those things out loud.

"No," Ethan says. "I don't know how much parent drama you can cope with right now, so all I said was that I was worried about you being on your own. But Oscar, we need to get you help."

The popcorn ceiling is an old friend. The cobwebs in the corner by the front door. The water stain that looks like an evil clown riding a dragon. I have stared at this ceiling for hours, alone in this house. The ceiling asks for nothing, wants for nothing. The ceiling just is.

"Oscar?" Ethan says.

They are waiting for me to say something. So I start talking.

"A couple of years ago, I joined this support group for shooting victims and their families. It's supposed to be therapeutic, but having a mom tell you how her five-year-old daughter was shot while wearing her favorite purple dress and she didn't know what to bury her in since the dress was covered in blood . . . it was goddamn depressing.

"Dr. Bergstrom said I should stop going to the meetings because they weren't helping. THANK. GOD. I see him a couple of times a month to work on my anxiety and PTSD. He put me on antidepressants, but I got a bad reaction to them, so I began self-medicating with marijuana. Things are more bearable—a nice, cozy haze—when I get baked. So yeah, I get baked a lot.

"I got baked so much that I pretty much stopped going to school. I had to get at least a 2.5 average last semester or I was told not to bother coming back to school in January because there's no way I could bring my GPA up high enough to graduate. Spoiler . . . I did not get at least a 2.5 average."

"You could get a GED," Matt says.

I burst out laughing. Ethan looks like he wants to throttle Matt, but that's what I like about Matt. His total lack of bullshit. If there's a problem, there must be a solution. It's the wrong problem, but you got to start somewhere.

"I should, Matty," I say. "I've already been kicked out of three different schools. Fuck high school. You don't need it, right? I'll homeschool it. Let's go get burgers."

I stand up. The two of them look at me. Matt's wide-eyed like he's shocked I agreed with him. Ethan's eyes are narrowed, like he's trying to read my mind. I never noticed how much he looks like Aunt Sylvia until he does that. It's a squinty but all-knowing, measure-you-up-and-find-you-wanting stare.

"You didn't want to deal with Gibbs's letter and you still don't," Ethan says. "You were thinking suicide might be better than dealing with it. But Matt and I, we're not mental health professionals. You need to call your therapist."

I grow cold inside. Ethan is close, so close to hitting the target. I've actually spent eight years not dealing with how Gibbs fucked up my life. Eight years of holding on to the pain, like Raveena said. I'd keep getting high to stop feeling anything. If I call Dr. Bergstrom now, I have to deal with all this shit that's been piling up. "I'm not ready for that."

"No one's ever ready to deal with trauma," Ethan says softly. "That's the whole point of getting help."

Oh damn, I'm going to cry again. I blink fast to keep the tears inside my fucking eyeballs. I am so, so tired of living with myself. That's why I bought the gun, no matter what lie I told myself about Gibbs.

"It's okay to be scared, Oscar," Ethan says, still in that soft voice. "It's okay to talk about it. Would it help if I called Dr. Bergstrom for you?"

My hand seems to have a will of its own as I give my phone to Ethan. He scrolls through my contacts until he finds Dr. Bergstrom.

He makes the call. "Dr. Bergstrom? My name is Ethan Shapiro. I'm Oscar Vargas's cousin. Oscar is in crisis and needs to speak to you."

Ethan hands the phone back to me with an encouraging smile. I take the phone and look at it like I've never seen it before.

"It's okay if you want some privacy," Ethan says. "How about you go to your bedroom?"

I nod dumbly as I walk down the hallway. I close the bedroom door behind me. My hand is so sweaty I can barely hold the phone.

"Oscar? Are you there?" I hear Dr. Bergstrom say.

"Yeah." I lean against the door.

"Whenever you're ready, Oscar."

I just start bawling. I'm crying until snot runs down my nose and I can taste the salty goo on my lips. I wipe it with the back of my hand, but I'm still crying. Now there's snot all over my face and my hand. I'm such a fucking disaster. I don't know how long I cry for, but every now and then I hear Dr. Bergstrom throw in a "Take your time, Oscar" or a "Let it out."

Finally, a shuddering sigh comes out of me. I realize I'm sitting on the floor now, my back still against the door. I wipe my nose with the sleeve of my T-shirt.

"Oscar?" Dr. Bergstrom asks gently. "Would you like to talk now?"

"I'm sorry, Dr. Bergstrom. I've been a shitty patient. I half-assed the action plans. All I wanted was to get high and be as numb as humanly possible. I didn't want to do the work because I didn't want to feel the pain, but the truth is, I feel the pain all the time and I can't do it anymore. I can't."

"Are you having suicidal thoughts, Oscar?"

"Yeah." I barely breathe the word.

"I can help you, Oscar. Let me help you."

"How?" I hiccup the word. I don't want to cry again.

"Start by telling me when you began having the suicidal thoughts."

"I got a letter a couple of weeks ago. From the shooter. He wanted me to—I dunno, get even? He says he's not asking for forgiveness because he doesn't deserve it, but maybe if I kick his ass or whatever, he thinks he'll feel better? I mean, it's all fucked up. He gave me his address and wrote that he'd be alone on New Year's Day. Today."

"And what did you do?"

"I bought a gun."

"Where's the gun now, Oscar?"

"My cousins have it. I wanted to protect myself."

"How were you going to protect yourself?"

"By . . . by killing myself." My voice is so rough and low that I don't even recognize it.

"This letter from Gibbs was forcing you to confront your trauma in a very immediate way. I can understand the fear you must have had when you received it."

"I kept the letter in my pocket, thinking about it. But I don't want to see him. I don't want anything to do with him. I'm never going to forgive him."

"Oscar . . ." Dr. Bergstrom is quiet for a moment. "We've talked about forgiveness before. Forgiveness doesn't mean forgetting what he did or excusing the harm he caused. It means making a choice to free yourself from the negative feeling you have toward him."

"Forgiving is letting go of the pain?" I ask in a whisper.

"Exactly so, Oscar," he says. "During our sessions, I've been giving you tools to cope with your trauma, but you haven't been ready to use them yet. I think you're ready now, Oscar. You should consider this your chance to confront your trauma on your terms, not on his."

I take a shaky breath. Maybe . . .

MATT

Ethan plops on the couch next to me after Oscar goes to his room.

"How did you know to do all that?" I am impressed by Ethan's calm and the way he handled the situation.

He rests his head on the back of the couch and stares at the ceiling like Oscar did. "Do you think that water stain looks like a Demogorgon riding a surfboard?"

"Ethan!" I say, not looking up at the water stain, because I know it will distract me until I figure out what it looks like.

He finally turns his attention to me. "I'll tell you, but you can't let anyone know."

"Not even Oscar?"

"I'll tell Oscar later, when it's the right time."

"I promise I won't tell."

"Last year, Jiwon was super stressed out about getting first chair and grades and being the perfect Korean daughter. She started having panic attacks and then started hurting herself. She didn't tell anyone, not even me. Her avoidance and denial tactics were almost as highly developed as Oscar's. But I eventually figured out what was going on. It took her awhile to forgive me because I told her parents, but she got the help she needed."

"Oh." I never know what to say when people share intensely personal stories. People may think I don't care, but I'm more afraid of saying the wrong thing.

"I don't mean to sound judgey, but why is mental illness such a stigma to Christians? Is it because they think they're being punished for some sin? Jiwon's parents thought that. They wanted to have their pastor pray over her. They thought faith alone should cure her. I did a ton of research and showed them the benefits of mental health treatment. Yes, pray all you like, but get her medical help, too. If she broke an arm, you wouldn't just pray, you'd take her to a doctor. You can do both and it's fine with God."

He's right. That approach is both logical and spiritual. Yet as I think about it, I realize that Pastor Timothy has never spoken about mental illness, at least not as something people in his congregation may be struggling with. He does, however, speak frequently about carrying your own cross.

"There are those who may think it's punishment, but I think it's because suffering is seen as an honor," I say. "Christ suffered for us, so we should be able to bear any suffering we have with His help."

"See, that right there makes no sense. If Christ suffered for you, then you shouldn't have to suffer at all."

"Of course we're going to suffer. We live in the fallen world. But we trust in Christ to see us through the suffering. We learn from our suffering."

"Jew here! Don't get me started on suffering. I've said it before and I'll say it again, Christians are weird."

It is possible that we are weird since *weird* can mean "other-worldly." We are to be *in* the world, but not *of* it. But Ethan has mentioned something that I want to know more about. "Can you send me that research you did for Jiwon's parents?"

Ethan narrows his eyes. He looks like Aunt Sylvia when he does that. "Sure. But why do you—"

"Ethan! Dr. Bergstrom wants to talk to you!" Oscar shouts from down the hall.

Ethan jumps off the couch and is gone before he can finish asking why I want the research. I put my head back against the couch and look up at the water stain. It's definitely the Statue of Liberty half-buried in the sand.

OSCAR

Ethan says a lot of *uh-huhs* as he talks to my therapist. I know Ethan will follow through with whatever he tells him to do.

It was a relief to finally tell everything to Dr. Bergstrom. But am I really ready to forgive Gibbs? Am I ready to forgive myself?

ETHAN

"Call me anytime for anything. But you being there for Oscar is what he needs the most right now," Dr. Bergstrom says.

"Uh-huh."

"It takes practice to know when to nudge Oscar toward good choices and when to let him get there on his own. Follow your instincts."

"Uh-huh."

"You have a good head on your shoulders, Ethan. You'll do fine."

"Thanks, Dr. Bergstrom," I say as we wrap up the call. I am trying to stay calm, but my heart is beating faster than if I had a venti cappuccino.

I keep thinking about how much I messed up when I confronted Jiwon about her self-harm. I yelled at her, I took her anger personally, I made her feel responsible for her own pain. No wonder she didn't talk to me for two months. I should have been a better friend and searched the Internet on how to encourage someone to get therapy before I confronted her. At least I didn't make that mistake with her parents.

I take a deep breath like I've seen Matt do. I take another one. The tension in my chest starts to loosen up.

I look around Oscar's room. There's an unmade bed, clothes on the floor, the usual stuff you'd find in a guy's bedroom. But along one wall are metal shelves filled with crates of old vinyl albums. A vintage stereo system sits in the middle.

"All those albums were your dad's?" I ask in awe.

"Most of them." Oscar sounds proud to show them off. "I've bought some vinyl at local record shops. Stuff I thought he would like."

For the first time, I really look at Oscar. He seems to have loosened up too. He's standing straight instead of slouching. The haunted look on his face isn't exactly gone, but it's joined by . . . hope, maybe?

"Cool." That easy teasing we had earlier seems to have disappeared, but I think it's been replaced with something else. Something stronger.

"Thanks," Oscar says, "for making me call Dr. Bergstrom."

"I didn't *make* you—"

"Yeah, yeah, whatever it was, it helped. Shut up and let me thank you."

I smile. "All righty, then. You're welcome."

My phone pings. I want to ignore it, but Oscar gives me a slight nod like it's okay to check.

"Uh, my mom says she's texted and left a voicemail for your mom about you staying with us but hasn't heard anything back yet," I say.

"Yeah, that's my mom," Oscar says. "She'll get around to it eventually."

"So Aunt Elena isn't home much?" I never considered how much Oscar was literally alone.

Oscar pulls his T-shirt over his head. I wasn't going to say anything to him, but I did notice the streaks of snot on the sleeve. "Not much," he says, exchanging his black T-shirt for a gray one.

"I have a theory," I say, "about our moms."

"Yeah?"

"The way they are, it's because of how they grew up. Grandpa Manny was a super social drinker, customers loved him, and it was good for business. But he was a high-functioning alcoholic and no one would admit it. If he forgot a birthday, it was because he'd been so busy at the restaurant. If he was a yeller, everyone knows that chefs are temperamental. If he came home so drunk that he hit his head on the planter and needed stitches, well, that only happened once."

"My mom never really talks about him."

"My mom couldn't wait to leave home because she was tired of pretending everything was fine. Plus, she was the oldest and expected to take care of everything. So that's what she does. She makes shit happen."

"I've noticed how she takes names and kicks ass. She got Grandma buried in record time."

"And Aunt Norma is the middle child, the peacekeeper of the family. Doesn't want to make waves, makes excuses instead. And your mom is the golden child, the one who's successful to cover up the shame of growing up in an alcoholic home."

"You're saying our family has been fucked up for a couple of generations now?"

"I'm saying dysfunction can be generational, but it doesn't have to be. My mom went to therapy after Grandpa Manny died. She wanted to heal from the anger and resentment she had. We can change, Oscar. We can do better. Including your mom."

Oscar rolls up his dirty T-shirt into a ball and dunks it into his laundry hamper. "God, I hope so."

We each wait awkwardly for the other one to say something. I can only think of one thing. "How about we finally eat?"

"Sure." Oscar smiles, a real smile, not a smirk or a shit-eating grin, and he looks so young. I think I'm finally seeing the real Oscar.

MATT

I flip over a grilled-cheese sandwich on the griddle. I have made up my mind. Ethan and Oscar won't like my decision, but I think it's the right one. Ethan seems to know how to handle Oscar. I've seen how they have bonded during this trip. They were trying not to hurt my feelings when they left me out of their waffle outing or whatever it was, but I know I'm a third wheel.

And then there's The Reckoning. I don't know how to reconcile what I feel God wants me to do and what my parents want me to do. But if I go on alone, I'll have the rest of the drive to think about what to say to Dad.

"That smells fucking amazing," Oscar says. He and Ethan take seats at the kitchen table and watch as I finish cooking.

"It's only grilled cheese sandwiches with canned artichoke hearts and frozen spinach." I scoop up each sandwich with the spatula and put it on its own plate.

"Aunt Norma taught you how to make that?" Ethan asks.

"It's part of my homeschooling. Once you know the basics, you can improvise with what's on hand, and that's what was on hand." I put the plates on the table.

"What other basics did Aunt Norma teach you?" Ethan asks.

"Scrambled eggs, spaghetti, tortillas, chocolate chip cookies, simple things like that."

"Can you be my personal chef?" Oscar asks as he picks up his sandwich.

Now may not be the best time to tell them my decision, but I don't think there will be a best time. I rush out the speech I practiced in my head while I was cooking. "You guys should change your flight and leave for Las Vegas tonight. I can do the rest of the drive on my own."

Oscar stops eating. "I ruin everything, don't I?"

"No, not at all," I say. "But I can't really contribute anything. You don't need me around."

"We went to the beach this morning," Ethan blurts out. "We didn't invite you because we thought you could use the extra sleep. But it was a shitty thing to do, not to include you. Because we're in this together until the end. Three amigos, right?"

I'm grateful that Ethan has told me the truth about this morning. But it doesn't change my resolve. "I'm fine with ending the road trip here if it helps Oscar."

"Why don't you ask Oscar what he wants to do?" Oscar says.

Part of me is selfish enough that I'm hoping he wants to continue the road trip.

"What do you want to do?" I ask.

ETHAN

Breaking into a cemetery is not on my top five hundred things I thought I'd be doing today. But it's what Oscar said what he wanted to do. So here we are, at Pleasant Dale, jumping the fence, which is really only a hedge.

Oscar turns on the flashlight, but keeps it on low. "It's over here."

Matt and I follow him. It's a short walk across green grass that doesn't belong in the desert. We pass headstones and statues and plaques. Under an oak tree that also doesn't belong in the desert, there is it. Uncle Gilbert's gravesite.

IN LOVING MEMORY

GILBERT BERNARDO VARGAS

APRIL 11, 1972—JANUARY 31, 2011

GREATER LOVE HATH NO MAN THAN THIS,

THAT A MAN LAY DOWN HIS LIFE FOR HIS FRIENDS.

JOHN 15:13

There are flowers, stuffed animals, and a few miniature American flags by the black granite headstone.

I remember being here years ago. Hundreds of people had shown up for the church service, including the press and a couple of politicians, but the cemetery had only allowed close friends and family near the gravesite. Oscar wore a suit that was too big for him and kept rubbing his eyes with his fists to keep from crying. Matt told Oscar he was praying for him, and I thought Oscar was going to punch him. I didn't say anything to Oscar because I didn't know what to say.

I told Aunt Elena I loved the Ursula K. Le Guin books she and Uncle Gilbert had sent me for Hanukkah. She hugged me for a solid two minutes. They were Uncle Gilbert's favorites when he was my age, she said, but Oscar wasn't much of a reader.

I bet I could have nerded out with Uncle Gilbert. Debated classic geek arguments like Kirk vs. Picard and which Doctor had the best regeneration.

I bet I would have liked him a lot.

MATT

Dear Jesus, let Your grace fill Oscar's heart and begin to heal him. Let him find the peace he seeks. Guide him on his journey and I pray that in the end, he finds You.

Thank You for all the blessings and traveling mercies during our time together.

And, please, Jesus, give me the strength to help Dad so he finds peace, too.

In Your name I pray, amen.

OSCAR

I'm sorry, Dad. You had the courage to die for others, but I haven't had the courage to live. I've made shitty use of the life you gave me. Maybe I thought I didn't deserve it. Maybe I don't. But I want to live now, Dad. I want to do things that will make you proud. I may not change the world like Mom's trying to, but I can at least change myself. That's a start, right?

I miss you every day.

ETHAN

"Oscar, do you visit your dad often?" Matt asks as we drive away from the cemetery in Oscar's Jeep.

"Once a year."

"When?" I hope he doesn't say on his birthday. That would be the saddest thing ever.

"Opening day."

"You mean like baseball?" I ask.

"Yeah, I mean baseball."

"Who leaves the flowers and teddy bears?" Matt asks.

"My dad's former students and their families. There's not as much stuff as there used to be," Oscar says. "They've moved on."

"That doesn't mean they've forgotten him," Matt says.

"Maybe not." Oscar takes a left turn I'm almost certain isn't the way we came.

"Where are we going, Oscar?" He wouldn't actually go to Gibbs's house, would he?

"I gotta do something." He sounds determined.

Matt and I exchange looks but don't say anything. We don't have to. Whatever Oscar has to do, we'll be there with him.

OSCAR

I pull into the Applebee's parking lot. "You guys can wait here."

Ethan unbuckles his seat belt. "Yeah . . . no."

I don't want an audience for this, but I know Ethan won't leave me alone. Thanks, Dr. Bergstrom. "Okay, okay," I say. "But don't ask me any questions about this. The short answer is that I'm a dick, but you already knew that."

Matt nods, but Ethan doesn't. "I make no promises."

I blow out an annoyed breath. "Well, let's go then."

We arrive at the hostess station and wait behind a crowd. The place is packed, and I remember it's New Year's Day. The smiley hostess finally gets to us.

"Party of three?" she asks.

"No, I'm looking for Kayla Acosta. She still work here?"

The hostess doesn't lose her smile, but her eyes are throwing me daggers like I'm a creeper. "And you are . . ."

"I used to go to Dobson High with her. I'm Oscar Vargas."

The smile is unyielding. "Sorry, Kayla isn't working tonight."

"Can you tell her . . ." I can't tell Kayla what I want to tell her through this smiley hostess. "You know, fuck it."

I push past Ethan and Matt and go out the door. But they're only a step behind me.

"What was that about?" Matt asks.

I stop and turn around to Matt. "You're the one who promised not ask any questions!"

"Then I'll ask," Ethan says. "What the hell was that?"

"I already told you, I'm a dick. I've been a dick to a lot of girls, but Kayla is the only one I made cry."

"Are you here to apologize?" a gentle voice asks.

There she is. Kayla Acosta stands in the parking lot behind Matt and Ethan, not more than five feet from me. Ethan pokes Matt in the ribs, and they walk out of earshot by the Jeep.

"The hostess said you weren't working tonight," I say.

"I'm not. I'm here with my family. You didn't answer my question."

Why am I here? I wanted to see her again. I can't tell her that, though. I try to think of the right words to say, but the silence stretches into infinity. If I don't say something soon, she's going to walk away.

"Yeah."

"Yeah, what?" she asks.

"I came to apologize. You tried to be my friend and I shut you out. I was mad at you for seeing the pain in me that I couldn't admit." I'm rambling. I need to get to the point. Is there a point? There must be, or I wouldn't be here. "You don't have to forgive me if you don't want to. But I wanted to say thank you for being you. You were always kind to me. I needed that more than I knew. I'm sorry. I'm sorry for hurting you."

"I always forgave you, Oscar. I'm glad you're starting to forgive yourself."

Now she's going to make me cry.

Without a word, she puts her arms around me. She's tiny, but her hug is fierce. It's an endless moment that I will keep locked away for the times when everything gets to be too much. She says a prayer, but I don't hear the words. I feel them. I feel her breath against my chest, and I think that this is what baptism should be.

Then she's walking back toward Applebee's. "God bless, Oscar."

ETHAN

"Hector sent me a text," Matt says as we pile back into the Jeep. "He'll drop off the Beast at your house in about ten minutes."

"Just enough time for one more stop," Oscar says.

"Where to now?" I ask. If Oscar's going to apologize to every girl he's pissed off, this could take all night.

Oscar doesn't say anything. He keeps driving for a few more blocks and then stops in front of a nondescript 1990s-style ranch house.

"Anyone got a pen or something?" Oscar asks.

Matt pulls a small notebook with a pen from his coat pocket. He hands the pen to Oscar. The notebook has *Ideas* written across the front.

Oscar takes Gibbs's letter out of his jeans pocket and scribbles on the back.

"Wait, this is Tanner Aaron Gibbs's house?" I ask. "You're actually going to see him?"

Oscar gets out of the Jeep without answering me. He stands for a long time looking at the house.

Matt and I join him. We don't say anything. We simply look

at the house together. There's a light on, but I can't see anything through the curtains.

Oscar squares his shoulders. He walks toward the front door. We follow him. Once he reaches the door, he stops like he's frozen.

Each second that passes feels like another weight dropping on my chest. I can't imagine what Oscar is feeling. I remember what Dr. Bergstrom said about nudging Oscar toward good choices but letting him get there on his own. My instincts tell me this is definitely one he needs to get to on his own.

"Is this what you really want to do?" I ask.

"Yeah."

He takes the letter and shoves it through the mail slot in the door. Matt pats him on the shoulder. Oscar turns around and heads for the Jeep. We follow him.

MATT

INT. RANCH HOUSE — FOYER — NIGHT

The FOLDED LETTER lies on the tiled floor of the foyer.

THE LIVING ROOM is almost dark, just one lamp lit on a side table. Slouched on the couch is TANNER AARON GIBBS, 21, blond hair, thin beard, slightly overweight. He's asleep with a *Walking Dead* comic resting on his stomach.

He wakes up with a start.

He looks around the room. Doesn't see anything.

He settles in on the couch, about to go back to reading, when he sees the FOLDED LETTER on the floor.

He gets off the couch and walks toward the letter.

SOCKS and FOLDED LETTER fill the screen until a HAND comes down and picks up the letter.

He unfolds it. He knows this letter. It's in his own handwriting.

He turns the paper over. There is someone else's writing on it.

He reads it.

He rushes to the window and pushes away the curtains to look out at the street. It's empty except for a FALCON flying away.

OSCAR

Here's the thing I've learned about forgiveness—you give it because of who you are, not because the other person deserves it.

ETHAN

We drive back to Oscar's house in silence. I stare at my phone, trying to think of what to say to Levi. I want to tell him about Oscar. I want his advice. I want his comfort. I want to apologize.

How hard is that, to type the words *I'm sorry*?

Me:
I have a theory.
I can flirt.
I can banter.
I can kiss you a thousand times.
But I don't know how to be a boyfriend yet.
Especially a boyfriend that's miles away from you.
The last thing I want is to be clingy
or needy or controlling.
I guess that's the last three things.
But you know what I mean.
I want us to work. SO. MUCH.
I miss you.
I'm sorry. ☹

I wait for a reply.

MATT

The Beast cruises to a stop in front of Oscar's house. A white pickup truck follows behind. Hector gets out of the Beast and hands me the keys. He's changed out of his work clothes and wears a baggy T-shirt and long shorts with athletic slides and white socks.

"*Oye*, the belt's been replaced, but the water pump has some deposit buildup. You wanna do a coolant flush when you get to where you're going."

"But it's okay to drive?" I ask.

"Yeah, but your heater won't work great."

"That's fine. We have extra blankets."

Hector chuckles. I hand him the hundred dollars, which he puts in the pocket of his shorts. He climbs into the passenger seat of the pickup truck. "You got any more repairs you need, come on by." He waves as they drive off.

I look at the Beast. Hector rinsed it off with a hose, washing away the dust and grime it collected over the past few days. I'm relieved to have it back. For the first time, I feel as though the Beast is *my* car. Feeling affection for an inanimate object seems odd, but now I understand why people name their cars.

"Welcome back, Beast."

ETHAN

"Should I change our flight?" I ask Oscar. He's digging through his closet, tossing his bong and other paraphernalia into a garbage bag. "If we're not going to Albuquerque, we can still catch the last flight to Las Vegas tonight."

"Do you want to change it?"

"It's not up to me. It's what you—"

"Answer the question." He chucks the bag into the trash can by his desk.

"I'd kinda like to stay with Matt." It's only been two days, but we've been through a lot together. It doesn't seem right to end it here.

"Me too." Oscar sits next to me on his bed. "We owe it to him, you know?"

"Yeah. Plus, I like hanging out with you guys."

"Me too." He's about to punch me on the shoulder, but he stops. He leaves his fist out, though. "Gonna leave me hanging?"

I give him a fist bump.

"I'm sorry for being such a dick to you and Levi when we were leaving Berkeley," he says.

I remember the honking, but mostly I remember the ache of saying goodbye. "I'm the one who fucked up, Oscar."

"What do you mean?"

"I overreacted when Levi sent me a photo of him at a New Year's Eve party. He was with a guy—a friend he's known since he was a kid and who's straight. It'd be like if Levi got mad at me for taking a photo with Jiwon. But I weirded out and basically accused him of liking Jake more than me."

"You're not perfect? Holy shit, what are we going to do now?" He slaps his hands on his thighs.

"I'm serious, Oscar. I had a theory Grandma was looking out for me in heaven, arranging it so I could meet Levi, and I messed it all up."

"I thought you didn't believe in heaven."

"Grandma believed in her version of heaven, and I want her to have that."

"Fair enough. But here's a theory for you. What if Grandma is looking out for all of us?"

"That is a really good theory," I say, because it is. "But how does that help me with Levi?"

"Did you apologize to him?"

"Yes, but I haven't heard anything back."

"Keep apologizing. You and Levi are too damn cute not to be together."

MATT

I pick up the box of bullets from under the onions in the vegetable bin. The box is full.

I take the gun and the ammo outside to the Beast. We decided that it's best if I kept the gun and disposed of it responsibly in Santa Fe. The police have a buyback program and Oscar said I could keep the Amazon gift card.

I open the trunk and unzip my suitcase. I pull out one of my shirts to wrap the gun in. A baggie falls on the ground.

I pick it up.

Even though I have never seen marijuana in person before, I know what this is. Did Oscar put it there by mistake? Is he giving it to me?

It doesn't matter. I stuff the baggie in my back pocket and finish packing up the gun and ammo. Once I'm done, I go to the bathroom and flush the marijuana down the toilet. Legal or illegal, it's not for me.

When I enter Oscar's bedroom, he's stuffing clothes into a duffel bag while Ethan sits on the floor, looking through the crates of vinyl records.

"The Beast is ready to go," I say.

"Thanks for taking care of all the gun safety shit, Matty," Oscar says.

"I'm glad I can help."

"Don't you have to get the gun re-registered or something before you take it?" Ethan asks.

"You don't have to register guns in New Mexico," I say.

"Or in Arizona," Oscar says.

"That's messed up," Ethan says.

"It's all messed up," Oscar says. "A few years ago, I was at a hearing at the Arizona State Senate about making background checks mandatory at gun shows. Gibbs's dad got all his guns at gun shows, and he had two domestic violence convictions, which meant he wouldn't have passed a background check. At first, the senators blew smoke up my ass about how my father was a hero and how honored they were to have me there. I told them they were a bunch of chickenshits who'd rather take NRA money than protect lives. They thanked me and told me I could leave."

"I remember that was on the news." I also remember how angry Dad was at Aunt Elena for indoctrinating Oscar in liberal propaganda.

"It got play on national television for a nanosecond but made zero difference in actually doing anything," Oscar says. "Gun control advocates like my mom go on news programs and speak before Congress, they march, they start foundations, they try to make a difference. But it will never be enough. Fucked-up people will always find a way to get a gun because the NRA buys politicians to block any real reform."

"I've belonged to the NRA since I was twelve." Even as the words come out of my mouth, I wonder if I've been indoctrinated in Dad's views.

"What do you get for being a member?" Ethan asks.

I blink. There has to be something tangible I get for being a member. "A discount at the gun shop. And a membership card."

"And what exactly do you shoot?" Ethan asks.

"Rabbits, mostly."

"Wait, wait, you kill little bunny rabbits?" Ethan says.

"They're jackrabbits. They can cause serious damage to crops and rangeland used by other animals like bighorn sheep. It's population control."

"Do you enjoy killing them?" Ethan asks, a look of dismay on his face.

I've been asked this question before, so I'm prepared. "I enjoy the accuracy of a clean shot. The animal doesn't even know it's been hit before it's dead. And it serves a greater good."

"I know you and Uncle Dennis hunt," Oscar says. "But hunters don't need goddamn semiautomatic weapons. Does the government stop them from being sold? No. Let's sell kids bulletproof backpacks instead. How fucked up is that?"

"Ruby learned 'the silent game' in her kindergarten class, which is how they teach little kids lockdown procedures," Ethan says.

"The first time my school had active-shooter training, I was in the sixth grade and I shit my pants," Oscar says. "Shit them like I had the runs. My mom ripped the principal a new one because he didn't give her advance warning. Uh, you think maybe you should tell the family of a shooting victim beforehand? The principal apologized, but my mom pulled me out of that school and put me in another one that did notify her whenever an active shooter drill was scheduled. She'd take me out of school for the day and we'd go to the movies or the park or something. It was kind of nice. Then her first book came out and she wasn't always around on drill days, so I would stay home and play Mario Kart."

"Even in high school, lockdowns can be scary," Ethan says. "Because part of your brain is thinking, 'Maybe it's not a drill this time.'"

"I've never had active-shooter training since I'm home-schooled." I remember the chapter headings in Aunt Elena's latest book. "The Lockdown Generation." "The Post-Traumatic Stress Generation." This isn't a discussion I'm prepared for. I never even considered that homeschooling has protected me from experiencing what most other students have had to deal with.

But even though I may not have gone through an active-shooter drill, I do know what fear is, and fear can make you angry. I understand Oscar's anger. "Guns are a right, but they're also a responsibility. I make no excuses for people who fail that responsibility."

"You got to hold them accountable, then," Oscar says as he zips up his duffel bag.

"'They profess to know God, but by their actions they deny him. They are detestable, disobedient, unfit for doing anything good,'" I say. "Titus 1:16."

"Oh, I like that one," Ethan says.

I smile. I hate having to say good-bye. But it's time. "I can drive you guys to the airport—"

"Ethan and I were talking. We're not going to abandon you, Matty. We're going to ride to Albuquerque together. You guys . . . you guys are all I've got right now."

I have never been a hugger. It's not something I'm comfortable with. So I don't hug Oscar. But I want to.

OSCAR

"Are you sure you want to drive?" Matt asks as he hands me the keys to the Beast.

"I'm good. Driving will help keep me focused." I buckle my seatbelt so he won't try to oust me from the driver's seat. "It's my turn anyway."

"It's my turn, actually," Ethan says from the back seat. "I haven't done any driving since we left Berkeley."

"Give me until, I dunno, Gallup. That's just past the state line, right?"

"Close enough," Matt says.

"Then you can do the last leg," I say to Ethan. "We should roll in with plenty of time before our flight leaves."

"As long as there isn't another accident or snow or ice on the road—"

"Matty, chillax. Time to crank it up and get this show on the road." I find the local oldies station and blast Queen's "We Are the Champions."

Ethan starts humming along. After a moment, Matt joins him. I pull away from the curb as the chorus starts. We all belt it out and for once, instead of feeling like the loser, I feel like maybe I could be a champion of the world.

ETHAN

Jiwon:

Where have you been????

Me:

Things got intense with Oscar.

He's coming home with me.

Jiwon:

Whoa. That's unexpected.

Me:

He's really struggling with his mental health.

I'm going to need your help.

Jiwon:

What can I do?

Me:

Talk to Oscar.

About what you went through.

Jiwon:

I don't know if I'm ready to share
my story like that, E.

Me:

He needs as many people on
his side as he can get.

Jiwon:

What have you told him about me?

Me:

That you're my bestie.
You can tell him as much or as little as
you want about everything else.
But I want him to meet someone who's
come through the other side.

Jiwon:

Mental health is more complicated than that.
What's working for me now may not work later
and Oscar needs to find his own balance.
I don't know how much help I'd be.

Me:

Just listening to him would help.
So start with that and maybe then
you'll want to tell him your story.

Jiwon:

E . . .
I'll think about it.

Me:

Thanks, J. You are my favorite person.

Jiwon:

Luv you.

Me:

Luv you too.

MATT

"Matty, what's the deal with your dad?" Oscar asks.

My jaw tenses. We've been listening to a triple play of Queen on the radio and then this question comes out of nowhere. I don't know how to answer it. I don't want to answer it.

"Is he still stuck in Denver?"

I let out a breath. I was too literal with Oscar's question. He's making small talk. We've had too much big talk already.

"Yes."

"That blows."

"At least he can walk around and stretch in the airport," I say.

"He's got a bad back, right?" Oscar asks.

"Yes, from the long hauls. He was gone a lot when I was growing up, but it was always a treat when he came home because he'd have presents for me from his travels."

"Did you ever go with him?" Ethan asks.

"During the summers I would, starting when I was ten. We visited a lot of Walmart warehouses. But I'd read out loud from atlases and other books with interesting facts about the places we were driving through."

"That sounds nice," Oscar says.

"It was," I say. "But he's been on disability for the past two years."

"Does the pain make him depressed?" asks Ethan.

Ethan has figured out why I wanted the research he did for his friend. "Sometimes."

"Is he taking any meds for the pain?" Ethan asks.

"Over-the-counter drugs. He refuses to take opioids."

"He should try weed," Oscar says. "It would mellow him out a lot."

"That's actually not a bad idea," Ethan says.

"The likelihood of that is low," I say.

"Does he have mood swings or anger issues?" Ethan asks.

"Sometimes. But it's not as though he's abusive." I don't tell Ethan about how when Dad yells, his face turns red, spittle collects in the corners of his mouth, and he clenches his fists. When that happens, he goes to the garage to pray. He comes out after he's calmed down and apologizes for his temper. It's been happening more often, at least a few times a month. I was glad to start taking classes at the community college to get out of the house for a while.

"There are different types of abuse," Ethan says. "Someone can be emotionally abusive and it still hurts. Grandpa Manny was emotionally abusive because he was an alcoholic."

"I knew he drank," I say. "I knew my mother didn't like it. I've never really thought about how much his drinking affected her." She was probably trying to protect me, but I wish she would have shared more with me.

"Even if you don't think your dad is being emotionally

abusive, he still needs to get help for his depression because it's affecting the whole family," Ethan says.

"Dude, even I know he needs help," Oscar says.

"I understand that now," I say. "The difficulty will be getting him to agree. He'll say that he doesn't need help, that he's praying about it. And with Grandma Lupe's passing and Mom opening a restaurant, he'll say it's not the right time to deal with it."

"What about Aunt Norma?" Oscar asks. "Could she convince your dad to get help?"

"In a Christian household, the wife is submissive to the husband."

"That would not go down in my house," Ethan says.

"And I'm not in the greatest position to tell my dad he needs help when I disobeyed him by going to California. I've broken his trust, and I'll have to rebuild it before he'll listen to me."

"How much trouble are you in?" Oscar asks.

"I don't know. I've never done anything like this before. But my chance of ever going to film school is gone."

"Matt, you can't make your dad get help for his depression, but you can still approach him and let him know you're concerned about him," Ethan says. "And it's obvious that film school is God's plan for you. You've got to trust God it's true and have faith that your parents will understand."

"Thank you, Ethan," I say. I pray he's right.

OSCAR

"Ethan," I say, "are you sure you want to be a dentist? You should be a therapist or something. It's less gross than sticking your hands in a person's mouth."

He chuckles. "Hadn't really thought about it."

"I think it's your—what's the fancy word for job, you know, like the job you're meant for?"

"Vocation," Matt says.

"Yeah, vocation. You care about people and shit."

"Don't know if it's a career for me, but I'll do whatever I have to for the people I care about. Even if it's something they'll hate me for. At least for a while."

"Ethan," I say, glancing back at him in the rearview mirror, "I don't hate you."

"Yeah, I know," he says, smiling. "We're cool."

"Imma pull my shit together. I got to think about the future here. It's scary as fuck."

"First get your GED," Matt says, "then maybe a gap year to think things through."

"Yeah, a gap year. It'll make my mom less stressed out if I have a plan."

"You could be a peer counselor," Ethan says. "I think you care about people, too, in your own way."

"Dude, nobody should take life-coach shit from me."

"In time, you could do it," Ethan says. "You can't see it now, but you could."

It didn't seem possible, not even a few hours ago. But there it is, the future, waiting for me to catch up to it.

PART V

ALBUQUERQUE

MATT

"I thought the Beast was fixed," Ethan says from the back seat. "I'm freezing. I'm going to die of hypothermia." He has one of Grandma Lupe's crocheted afghans draped over his head as he huddles underneath it.

"It's as cold as balls, but you don't hear me complaining," Oscar says. He still wears his hoodie, but he now has a black puffer jacket over it.

"Sorry about the heater, Ethan," I say, "but thank God we've gotten this far without something else going wrong."

I remember when I first saw the falcon watching us at Grandma's gravesite, it reminded me of God watching over all of us. That's what the falcon means to me, a reminder that wherever we go, God will be there for us.

And I've been thinking about what Ethan said about trusting God that my calling to be a filmmaker is true. I've realized it's not up to me to convince my parents that it's true. They have to come to trust God about it on their own.

The little green pine tree that Oscar bought in Portland swings on the rearview mirror as the Beast takes a turn along the mountainous road. We're just past Payson in the Tonto National Forest. There are flashes of real ponderosa pines as the headlights sweep across them. Flecks of white lightly fall on the windshield. They are gone as soon as Oscar flicks on the windshield wipers. Even so, they are miracles of God's creation. They are promises of renewal.

"Is that snow?" Ethan asks.

"It is," I say. "'Kindness is like snow—it beautifies everything it covers.'"

"Is that from a movie or the Bible?" Oscar asks.

"It's from the poet Khalil Gibran," I say.

"I like it."

"Me too."

"Me three," Ethan says. "But I'd like it more if the heater was working."

OSCAR

The fluorescent lights inside the convenience store are too bright and make my head ache. It's empty except for the tatted dude behind the counter. He gives me a nod as I hand him the cash for coffee and energy bars.

"Happy New Year," he says.

"Still?" I say, not thinking. "Shit, I thought it was tomorrow already."

To say it's been a long day is to think that twenty-four hours is the only way to measure it. It's been a loaded day. It's been a heavy day. It's been a surreal day. I wish I paid more attention to SAT vocabulary words because none of those are right.

He laughs. "Yeah, still. Too much partying?"

"Dude, you have no idea."

Tatted dude laughs again. "I got you," he says, nodding.

"Uh, sugar?" I ask.

He points to the coffee station behind me. "Sugar, creamer, whatever you need. Except that stevia crap. We don't carry that here."

"Cool, cool." I put the tray of coffee on the coffee station counter and stuff my pockets with packets of sugar and tiny tubs of creamer.

I'm relieved to pass the driving on to Ethan. I could use some shut-eye. Oh damn, I promised Matt I'd text Raveena and get him off the hook with Gwen. I forgot that with everything that went down. I turn on my phone for the first time in hours.

Two texts.

Both from Mom.

The first one is from this morning, and I ignored it.

Mom:
Happy New Year! Last chance to claim something of Grandma's.

The second one is from this evening.

Mom:
Talked to Sylvia and it's all good. Enjoy your time with Ethan! May stay in NY a few extra days now. Love you!

I know I'm going to have to eventually tell her about the letter. And the gun. But a few days away from Phoenix will help me figure out what I want to say to her. Then we can set up a family session with Dr. Bergstrom. It's not her fault she hasn't been around. It's not her fault she didn't notice I was circling the drain.

Except, it is. She's my mom. She can't help everyone but me. It feels like she's gone all the time because it's easier than being around me. I should write this down and read it to her during the session.

Then I remember all those mornings when she tried talking to me. She was reaching out and I was punishing her with my silence. And if I did say anything to her, I was lying. We have a lot to work out together, but at least now I'm willing to talk. I send her a text. Maybe she'll get that I'm trying.

Me:

Can you have Aunt Sylvia send me Grandma's vinyl records? Thx. Love you, too.

Then I shoot off a text to Raveena.

Me:

Go ahead and tell Gwen what an a-hole I am. Matt deserves a chance.

I wave to the tatted dude on my way out, balancing the coffee tray with one hand and opening the door with my hip.

"Happy New Year," I say.

ETHAN

Levi:

Hey.

> **Me:**
>
> Hey.

I haven't heard from Levi since I sent my apology hours ago. I hold my breath while I wait for his response.

Levi:

I'm new to this boyfriend thing, too. I didn't know what I did wrong. Then I realized I did nothing wrong.

> **Me:**
>
> It was me! All me! I'm such an idiot. I panicked when I saw you with Jake because I can't be with you and he can. I do trust you. I can't trust myself to know what to do.

Levi:

Be honest. Start with that.

Me:

I put so much pressure on myself that
everything has to be perfect all the time.
Like when you have a new car and you're so
paranoid you're going to scratch the paint.
I got worried that I'm not boyfriend material.
Why should you be with me when there
are smarter and cuter guys out there?

Levi:

That is ridiculous. No one can make me
laugh like you do. And like I said before, you
are adorbs. You're a good kisser, too.

Me:

Can you tell me I'm ridiculous
every time I doubt myself?

Levi:

It's the least I can do for my boyfriend.
And if we're going to have a successful long
distance relationship, we're going to have to set
some ground rules. We are exclusive, got that?

Me:

Absolutely!

Levi:

We can hang out with our friends
and not feel guilty.

Me:

Absolutely again!

Levi:

We have to be honest with each other,
even if it may be a tough discussion.

Me:

I promise. 🫶

Levi:

Good. That's all I've got. Now fill me in on how the
road trip is going. I need a previously-on montage.

Me:

I'm so relieved I can finally tell you about Oscar.
He's having a mental health crisis. He's willing to get
help, which is huge. He's coming home with me.
Truthfully, I'm feeling a little overwhelmed.

Levi:

You are one of the most capable people
I know. Oscar is lucky to have you. But
feel free to vent when you need to.

Me:

Thanks. That means a lot to me.

Levi:

Where are you now? Did the Beast get fixed?

Me:

Yes. Except the heater is broken. We're at a gas
station in Gallup, NM. So cold! ❄️ 🫁 ⛄

Levi:

Think warm thoughts. 🔥

Me:

I can see my breath and I'm sitting in the car.

Levi:

☕

Me:

When I say I want to live in a place that has
seasons, I mean only spring and fall.

Levi:

☼

Me:

I'd prefer a hug!

Levi:

HUGS

Me:

Warmer already. 😉

Levi:

How are you doing otherwise?

Me:

Exhausted. But we're almost to ABQ.

Levi:

Don't forget to take care of you!

Me:

More hugs?

Levi:

HUGS

I love you.

I gasp. I literally gasp. No one has said *I love you* to me before.
My family and Jiwon don't count. This is L-O-V-E, the kind
found in pop songs and Shakespeare and Maurene Goo novels.

Once I can breathe again, I text back.

Me:

I love you, too.

MATT

"I'm so going to have to pee," Ethan says as he hands me his empty coffee cup. "But at least I'm warm now."

Ethan drives more slowly than usual. There's only a light dusting of snow on the road, the kind that will melt once the sun rises, but I know he's not used to it. I put his empty cup in the plastic bag that I've started using for trash. I add a proper car trash bag to my list of things I need for the Beast.

My phone pings. I'm sure it's Mom checking up on me. I want to ignore it, but I know I can't.

Gwen:
Raveena told me everything.

"Guys?" I say, not sure what it is I want from them. But I show my phone to Oscar. "What do I say?"

"What? What am I missing?" Ethan says.

"Gwen knows we lied to her," I say.

"Does she sound mad?" Ethan asks.

"I don't know."

Oscar takes my phone and starts texting.

"What are you writing?" I try to grab it back, but the seatbelt chokes me as I reach behind me.

"Chillax, Matty. I got this."

"Oscar, please!" I try to pull more slack from the seat belt, but there is none. I let it choke me as I reach for my phone.

"Here," he says, handing back my phone.

I read the text he wrote.

"This is good," I say.

"I swear to God I will pull this car over unless you guys tell me what's going on," Ethan says.

I read Ethan the text. "'I'm sorry I let Oscar lie to you. Oscar's sorry, too. I'm glad I met you, but I understand if you don't want to talk to me anymore.'"

"Damn, Oscar, that is really good."

"Send it already, Matty."

"Wait a moment." I add one last thing to the text before I send it.

"What did you write?" Ethan asks.

"Romans 8:28."

"And that is . . .?"

"'And we know that in all things God works for the good of those who love him, who have been called according to his purpose.'"

"Smooth move, Matty."

"How long do you think it'll take before she texts back?" I ask.

"Depends on how upset she is," Oscar says. "An immediate 'Fuck off' means she's done with you. The longer she takes, the more she's thinking about how to let you off the hook while still letting you know you did a shitty thing."

"Since when do you know how the female mind works?" Ethan asks.

"I'm good at knowing how a pissed-off female mind works," Oscar says. "Usually they just want you to apologize. Usually I didn't care enough to. But I am sorry, Matty, that I made you lie for me. That's not cool."

I take a deep breath. The weight that has been pulling me down since last night is gone. Whatever happens with Gwen now will be based on truth, and that's all I wanted. "I forgive you, Oscar."

"Thanks, dude." He reaches forward for a fist bump. I oblige him.

ETHAN

The parking lot at Albuquerque International Sunport is almost empty. I easily pull the Beast into a spot. Of course the guys aren't awake to see it. Oscar fell asleep a while ago and even Matt nodded off before the *'85 Is Alive* mixtape finished playing. I liked having the time to think about things. Not that I came up with any answers, but not everything needs answers. Sometimes you need to figure out what the right questions are.

Matt snaps awake once I stop the engine.

"What time is it?" he asks.

"Three forty-seven a.m. We got a couple of hours to kill before our flight leaves."

Oscar stretches in the back seat. "Why don't we crash here until it's time to go?"

"You have to check in and go through security. The standard recommendation for domestic travel is to arrive at the airport two hours before your flight," Matt says.

"You're right, Matty. Want to make sure we beat the crowds."

"I need more coffee. And waffles. Do you think we can get waffles here?" I ask.

"I don't think anything will be open yet," Matt says.

"What snacks do we have left, Oscar?" I ask.

"Barbeque Corn Nuts, Funyuns, and Oreos."

"No real food?" Matt asks.

"The best food is stoner food," Oscar says.

"Take everything that isn't open yet and the bottled waters," I say. "We can drink them until we go through security."

"Sir, yes, sir!" Oscar salutes before he packs them up. He may be cracking jokes, but I know he's still super vulnerable. I have to remind myself that he's not my responsibility. I can support him as best I can, but it's up to him to follow through on treatment.

A blast of cold air rushes at me when I open the driver's door. "I didn't know I could be colder than I already was."

I hand over the keys to Matt, who doesn't even have his coat buttoned.

"I'm waiting with you guys," he says.

"Why? You can be warm and cozy at home before our plane takes off," I say.

"We see it through until the end, right, Matty?" Oscar says, climbing out of the back seat.

"There's no one home now, anyway," Matt says. "I'd rather stay with you."

"Crazy idea," I say, "but why don't you come with us to Vegas?"

"Hells yeah!" Oscar shouts.

Matt shakes his head. "I appreciate it, but I have obligations here."

"You know you're keeping us updated on the Gwen situation," I say as Oscar and I unload our bags from the trunk.

Matt blushes. "She hasn't texted me back. She probably never will."

"Matty, trust me, she's going to." Oscar slings his duffel bag over his shoulder and then punches Matt in the arm.

Matt rubs his arm. "We'll see."

They start to head toward the terminal. I slam the trunk shut. Then I pat it like it's a good dog. "Good-bye, Beast. Thank you."

OSCAR

The airport terminal is empty except for a janitor laughing at whatever he's watching on his phone and a couple of TSA agents powering down Dunkin' Donuts coffee. It takes Ethan about thirty seconds to fall asleep once we settle in the Meditation Room outside of baggage claim. Matt and I play Rock-Paper-Scissors-Lizard-Spock for a while, but that boy has skills and I finally give up.

I notice the time. We're going to have to get going soon. But this little spot of limbo has been what I needed. What's that word again? *Hope*. I have hope. My head feels clear. My soul feels light. If I have a soul. I'm not entirely sure about that one, but right now, it feels like I do and it's feeling like cotton-ball clouds. I'm going to have to work on my metaphors because that one sucked. Oh wait, that's a simile. Shit, I'm going to have to study if I want to pass the GED.

I join Matt at the Arrivals board. "Your dad's flight still delayed?"

"Actually, he should be arriving shortly before your plane takes off."

"That kinda worked out then, huh?"

"It might almost be called a miracle," Matt says.

"Tell him it's my fault we went to California. I don't mind if it takes the heat off you."

Matt cracks a smile. "That's a kind gesture, Oscar, but I think my dad needs a reckoning as much as I do."

There's so much I want to say and I don't know how. "Matt?"

"Yes?"

"Thanks. For everything." Is that really the best I can come up with?

"I think it's been a team effort."

I laugh. "A real *Fellowship of the Ring*, right?"

"Do I get to be Aragorn?"

"I don't know who that is, never saw the movie, but you can be whoever you want to be, Matty. I mean that. You're smart enough to find a way to get what you want."

"You too, Oscar." He puts his hand out for a handshake.

That is so fucking Matty. I shake it, but then pull him into a bro hug. "That's what brothers do."

Matt looks a little surprised when I let him go, but he's still smiling. "Okay."

We walk back to the Meditation Room. Matt nudges Ethan until he wakes up. "Ethan, it's time to go."

Ethan blinks twenty times before he puts on his glasses. "I'm up, I'm up." To prove it, he stands up from the wooden bench he'd been sleeping on.

Matt pulls him into a bro hug. "I've been told it's what brothers do."

Ethan smiles like he won the damn lottery.

Shit, I think I'm going to cry. I pick up my duffel bag and head for the security gate. "*¡Vamos!*"

MATT

INT. SUNPORT — PRE-DAWN

Matt exits the restroom. A motley group
of red-eyed travelers stagger into view
on their way out of baggage claim. Matt
recognizes one of them.

                    MATT
        Hi, Dad.

It takes a second for DAD to recognize Matt.

                    DAD
        Matt?

Dad drags his roller bag behind him as he
walks toward Matt.

                    DAD

    What are you doing here? Didn't Mom
    tell you that you didn't have to wait
    for me?

                    MATT

    I wanted to.

                    DAD

    Well, that's very considerate of you,
    son.

Long, awkward beat.

                    MATT

    How's your back?

                    DAD

    It could be worse.

Matt's phone PINGS. He takes it out of his
jeans pocket and looks at the text. We don't
see what it says, but it makes Matt smile.

                    MATT

    You know what, let's get waffles on the
    way home. There are some things I want
    to share with you.

                    DAD
          Sounds good, Matt.

EXT. SUNPORT — DAWN

Waves of purple and orange light break into
the darkness of the night sky.

A FALCON rises from the roof of the terminal
and flies toward the approaching sun.

                         FADE OUT.

               THE END

AUTHOR'S NOTE

Ethan likes Eighties music because I like Eighties music. Matt writes screenplays because I write screenplays. Oscar has trauma because I have trauma. While I deliberately made Oscar's trauma dramatic, there is no big trauma or small trauma. There is only *your* trauma.

The Substance Abuse and Mental Health Services Administration says more than two-thirds of children experience at least one traumatic event by the time they are sixteen years old. And this was before COVID-19.

If you have trauma, if you feel lost, if you feel alone, there are things you can do that may help you to feel better. Journal. Pray. Create. You don't have to have suicidal thoughts before you ask for help. And please don't ever feel as though you can't ask for help. So many people in the world want to see you thrive, and if it feels as though no one does, then maybe you haven't met them yet.

Here are a few places where you can connect with people who care:

Crisis Text Line:
Text HOME to 741741 or visit www.crisistextline.org

National Suicide Prevention Lifeline:
Call 1-800-273-TALK (8255) or visit
www.suicidepreventionlifeline.org

The Trevor Project:
Text START to 678-678 for Trevor Text or call
TrevorLifeline at 1-866-488-7386 or visit
www.thetrevorproject.org

If you'd like to help those who may be experiencing a mental health challenge, consider becoming trained in Mental Health First Aid.

Mental Health First Aid:
Visit www.mentalhealthfirstaid.org

I've done my best to express the truth of my characters, and any errors in the portrayals of mental health challenges are entirely my own.

ACKNOWLEDGEMENTS

Thanks and love to my entire family, especially my inspiration nephews: Warren, Andrew, Eric, William, and Tony. You may be related, but you're all so different that it inspired me to wonder, *What if you hadn't grown up together? What would you talk about? What would the dynamics be?* And that took me down the road to tell this story of family and faith and trauma and love. Special shout-out to Warren, whose insights were very much appreciated. Another special shout-out to Ronan—you are an inspiration in perseverance.

I am forever indebted to Lee & Low's New Visions Award for seeing the potential in *Boys of the Beast*. Tremendous thanks to my editor, Cheryl Klein, who helped me fulfill my vision of my boys. Oscar, Ethan, and Matt became deeper and more complete characters with your thoughtful questions and perceptive guidance.

To my beta readers: Laurel DiGangi, Laurie Young, Sara Bayles, and Wendy Jean Wilkins, thanks so much for your input and encouragement. You're amazing writers and brought a strong story sense and character-building skills to your notes. There will be more dim sum in our future.

To Kelli Joan Bennett, your support for my writing over the years has kept me going. *Collusions* lives!

To Carrie Firestone, thank you for being a mentor and letting me ask all the newbie questions I could think of. I am grateful for your willingness to lift others up.

To Tricia Lawrence, thank you for believing in me and my writing. I look forward to doing amazing things together. Special shout-out to Paula Yoo for introducing us.

To Henry, my violin expert, my grammar nerd, I will always choo-choo-choose you.